Born in 1969, Swiss author Jose fifteen novels across a range of for theatre and cinema. His wor cally acclaimed; it has won nume ...... adapted for film. Incardona's wor ..... translated into German, Italian, Korean, and Georgian, but this is his first book available in English. He resides in Geneva.

JOSEPH INCARDONA

Translated from the French by Sam Taylor

BITTER LEMON PRESS
LONDON

BITTER LEMON PRESS

First published in the United Kingdom in 2026 by
Bitter Lemon Press, 38 Earl's Court Square, London SW5 9DQ
www.bitterlemonpress.com

First published in French as *Stella et l'Amérique* by Éditions Finitude, Paris, 2024

Copyright © Éditions Finitude, 2024, by arrangement of Florence Giry Agency (FGA), Paris.

English translation © Sam Taylor, 2026

The translation of this work was supported by the Swiss Arts Council Pro Helvetia

A CIP record for this book is available from the British Library

PB ISBN 978–1–916725–256
eB USC ISBN 978–1–916725–263
eB ROW ISBN 978-1-916725-270

The authorised representative in the EEA is Easy Access System Europe:
Mustamäe tee 50, 10621 Tallinn, Estonia, gpsr.requests@easproject.com

Typeset by Tetragon, London
Printed and bound by CPI Group (UK) Ltd, Croydon CRO 4YY

swiss arts council
prohelvetia

CONTENTS

"They got to live before they can afford to die."

JOHN STEINBECK, *The Grapes of Wrath*

Stella wasn't exactly beautiful, and she wasn't too smart either. But you could trust her. She meant what she said. And when you think about it, that might be all you need in this life to become a saint.

So, not too smart and not exactly beautiful… but desirable? Oh yeah, she was certainly that. It was something in her attitude, her posture. The way she moved her hips. The way she looked at you. When Stella gazed into your eyes, you were the only man on earth. You were important. It didn't matter who or what kind of man you were: Stella looked at you with her innocent amber eyes, and you were alive.

She looked into you.

Deep inside you.

Those eyes penetrated your heart, your blood.

And made you feel alive.

So it was only natural that Stella became what she carried within her: the quantification of desire.

And when you think about it, that might be all you need in this life to become a whore.

I

ANNUNCIATION

1

That night—a night in June, with bats swooping around her hastily tied hair—she had waited for the tumult in her head (which she pictured as cold blue water crashing against a rock) to die down before she locked her RV and walked over to Santa Muerte's trailer. It wasn't far, a hundred yards or so, and she covered the distance quickly, her bare feet tickled by the springy grass growing in patches on the dry ground. Even so, she still had time to slap a dozen mosquitoes that were feasting on her bare arms, on her thighs as hard as love.

Stella Thibodeaux was nineteen: the age of martyrs. Although she wasn't sure the date of birth on her ID was correct. What she did know was that she needed to talk urgently with the woman who had taught her everything about men.

This same Santa Muerte had suggested to her that she could become a carnival follower. The old Mexican fortune teller, half her face disfigured by skin cancer, presided over a crystal ball inside her caravan. But she hadn't needed to be clairvoyant to guess that the carnival's shooting gallery would bring in clients with other things on their minds than getting their faces sticky with cotton candy.

Stella knocked three times on the polyester resin door. A muffled voice told her to come in. When the Mexican woman saw the girl moving toward her through the gloom, she coughed and lit up her thirty-ninth cigarette of the day.

The last nail in her coffin? Well, maybe, but it was already so full of nails that it weighed way more than her scrawny old body. She was almost ninety years old and barely a hundred pounds, but still death didn't want her. "I guess I just haven't talked enough shit down here yet," she told Stella once. "People need hope, you know, and when they run out of hope, they need lies, because lies are the only things that can keep them going."

Now the old woman looked up at her and asked: "What brings you here, *amorcita?*"

Santa Muerte spat in the plastic bowl at her feet. She wiped her mouth with a dirty handkerchief and took a gulp from a bottle of mezcal. Smoking unfiltered cigarettes and drinking mezcal was her way of trying to cut a long life short. The worm inside the bottle bobbed against her mouth before sinking back to the bottom. She licked her lips with her small black tongue.

"Sit down and talk, honey. I don't wanna keep my clients waiting."

"I didn't see anybody outside."

"Well, I talk with ghosts too, you know. Most of my work is invisible."

Stella sat on the uncomfortable wicker chair, its foam cushion flattened by thousands of tightly clenched asses. Hesitantly, almost reverently, she placed her transparent, blue-veined hands on the crystal ball.

"How do you see the future in this thing, Santa?"

"Imagination and empathy. Experience, too. So what's on your mind?"

"Okay. Um… well, it's happened again, Santa."

"You mean one of these *resorptions?*"

"Why do you call them that?"

"Because I don't like the other word that comes to mind. For God's sake, kid, spit it out!"

"One of my clients yesterday. He had some kind of disease on his face. What do you call it? Synopsis? Catharsis?"

"Psoriasis... Jesus, Stella, so you just take anyone?"

"It was you who told me never to turn down work."

"*Bueno.* Go on..."

"Well, we did what he came for, then he went away. And then tonight he comes back again and... there's nothing on his face. His skin's as perfect and smooth as a baby's butt."

"And?"

"And so he falls to his knees, weeping, and says I've cured him. *I* cured him, Santa, and I have no idea how this is happening."

The old woman took another swig of mezcal, and this time she sucked the little worm into her toothless mouth and swallowed it. Then she slammed down the bottle on the round table decorated with a doily that had once been white. Stella felt the crystal ball tremble under her hands.

"How many is that, Stella?"

"He's the third. Since the start of the month."

"What sign are you again?"

"Sign?"

"Your star sign, girl."

"My papers say I was born on September fourteenth."

"The Virgin. Hmm..."

"I don't understand, Santa."

"You know what, *querida?*"

"What?"

"There's a pretty good chance you're in deep shit, my love."

2

Robert Smith was married, with three children. His severe psoriasis had become a problem: in his marriage, at work, in every aspect of his life. His wife Helga would only have sex with him when the lights were out and her own face was buried in a pillow. Robert had worked the counter at a post office, but in the end he'd been demoted to the sorting office because he was scaring the customers.

Night had fallen now, but he didn't dare go home looking like this. So he drove through town randomly, the AC turned up full blast, and his fishing equipment, which he hadn't touched all day, in the trunk. He was going to have to explain to his wife how the miracle had occurred, and the consequence would be a divorce and alimony payments so steep he would end up sleeping in his car.

That Sunday morning, as he was driving toward Penholoway Bay for a solitary fishing trip, Robert had seen the young woman sitting outside her RV by the side of the road. Blonde hair, pale skin. He'd driven straight past, because he didn't go with prostitutes. But when he'd spotted her in his rearview mirror, getting up from her red plastic chair and stretching as she walked, he'd felt that urgent desire for purity, for a flawless body to lighten the burden of his ugliness.

Now his conscience weighed heavily on him. What was the point of his body being healed if his soul was scarred by guilt? Besides, he'd been baptized; now was the time to take advantage of that fact, to share the news of his deliverance, his skin washed clean of all sin.

In the parking lot, Robert Smith got out of his Chevy pickup and was hit in the face by the stifling heat before entering the prefabricated church that stood next to Taco Bell, the fast-food restaurant's neon bell ringing silently in the spot where the church's bell tower should have been. He took off his baseball cap, crossed himself, and read the name of the priest displayed near the stoup.

He sat on a pew and stared at the crucifix on the wall while he waited for the confessional to be vacated. It was surprising to him that he was able to confess his sins so late at night. Maybe the Church was adapting itself to the Age of Perpetual Connection? In any case, today had been an epiphany for Robert Smith.

He decided to stop trying to understand.

A little old woman came out of the confessional, and Robert wondered what she could still have to reproach herself for at her age.

Give the dumb questions a rest, okay, Bob? It's time to testify.

Robert Smith stood up and went to take his place inside the booth. He drew the crimson velvet curtain behind him. He could barely make out Father Brown's face behind the latticework. "I'm listening, my son," the priest said. His voice was as deep and stern as justice.

Father Brown was about to hear Robert Smith's confession.

From that point on, the world would never be quite the same again.

3

A tall, broad-shouldered man with a gray brush cut and a face carved deeply by experience, Father Brown was the kind of caricature who has lived a whole other life before taking refuge in asceticism. It would be an understatement to say he had witnessed the depths to which the human soul could sink, first as a former Navy SEAL in the Mekong Delta during the Vietnam War, then as a missionary in Sierra Leone and Rwanda during the massacres of the 1990s. No, darkness and horror were never far from his memory. *Homo homini lupus est*, as Thomas Hobbes wrote. Well, someone had to stick their finger in the dike to stop the promised flood from destroying humanity. Having swapped his M16 assault rifle for a Bible, Father Brown had gone to war armed with nothing but the Word of God. He had spoken, and—sometimes—people had listened. In his experience, confession was an effective means of combating the perfidious evil that lurked inside each human being. Sun Tzu had advised readers of his book *The Art of War* to know their enemy, and nothing Father Brown heard could surprise him. On the contrary, it was necessary to dive deep into confession, regret, and remorse, to probe the Great Fear of Death and the Quest for Meaning that sometimes make us lose our way. That was why he worked the night shift. Over the years, he'd noticed that the cover of darkness, and the tiredness it brought, tended to loosen men's tongues, offering a shortcut to the hidden verities of a mea culpa.

And now Father Brown was sitting at the counter of this dive bar, shoulders hunched as he stared into a glass of bourbon watered down by melting ice cubes. He'd just lit his first cigarette of the day, the late-night cigarette of a onetime chain-smoker who can't bear to quit completely. If you wanted a quicker, more efficient description of this character, you might think of Robert Mitchum in *The Night of the Hunter*. Not only the knuckles tattooed with LOVE and HATE, but also the Shakespearean dilemma that tormented him.

To tell or not to tell.

Now, here, seated on a gleaming chrome and aluminum barstool.

Fingers gripping a glass of whiskey dripping with condensation.

To tell or not to tell, goddamn it!

(Sorry, God.)

Someone appeared on the stool to his right: a woman in her fifties with crows'-feet around her eyes and lines on her face that suggested a life lived without bitterness. "I'm like the tide," she said. "High or low, I come back every night."

"Constancy is a quality I appreciate, Margot."

"Still haven't made your mind up?"

"I'm sixty-six, Margot. Close to the number of the beast… And in recent years, I've been trying to turn my back on sin. You know that."

"Whereas I prefer to look at the world through a shot glass darkly."

"You're not the problem here. You know that too."

"If you gave me a chance, I'd abandon it all. Just for the opportunity."

"What do you mean by 'all'?"

"What little remains to me."

"It's more than that, Margot."

"Okay, but don't forget. When the time comes, I'll be ready to love you. Will you keep that in mind?"

"I will, I promise. But right now I need to be alone. To think. I'm tormented by a Shakespearean dilemma, you see."

Margot didn't go far. She moved to the other end of the bar, where another single man was glad to have her company. He bought her a vodka and lime, and the night went on.

Father Brown loosened his dog collar with his index finger, which came out damp with sweat. A ceiling fan was spinning above his head, but the air in the room was as thick as a greasy steak. He knocked quietly on the countertop. The bartender looked up and made a movement with his chin that meant *What do you need?*

"An answer, Frankie. I need an answer."

Frankie Malone was a former boxer. At twenty-seven, he'd lost the middleweight Golden Gloves championship to Rudi Moreno in the seventh round. His life since then had been marked by the scars on his face and a mortgage on this establishment that he'd never pay off.

"Life's a bitch, and I blame Jesus," said Frankie, drying the glasses as he took them out of the dishwasher.

"Don't blaspheme," Father Brown replied.

"You need an answer, preacher? That's mine. Life's a bitch, and I blame Jesus."

4

Stella Thibodeaux was woken by a beam of sunlight as thin as a shaving of Parmesan. A conjunction of elements on both a human and a cosmic scale: the position of her face on the pillow, perfectly aligned with the angle of the sunlight filtered through the twisted blinds on the window of her motor home.

A single minute in a life. Opening her eyes. Looking around. The succession of events necessary just to be there, and to breathe.

Stella stretched. And even though she was alone in her RV, her baggy, sleeveless T-shirt gave a glimpse of her firm, delicate breasts, like a pair of Beurre Hardy pears: golden skin, juicy flesh, sweetly perfumed... a fragile fruit.

She lit her camping stove with a match, then boiled some water and drank a mug of Nescafé. The portable AC unit was humming near her bed. Stella sat on the miniature toilet seat and the jet of her urine hissed loudly against the tin bowl, which made her laugh, a sonic gleam that mingled with that of the sun, shining 92.9 million miles away.

Because that's life, right?

And the beauty of a world where a girl was pissing in the pale blue morning.

That was why you had to take what you could. With humility and gratitude.

With patience.

And as soon as Stella opened the door of her motor home, they were already there, waiting for her. Their sorrows were lifted, their faces heavy with hope now she had appeared. Men. Damaged, weakened, ugly men. Men who wanted to live without the shameful weight of this degradation that refused to grant them the elementary grace of a healthy body. A dozen men: tubercular, paraplegic, blind, sick and disabled in multiple ways. Some of them took grimy ten-dollar bills from their pockets and held them out to her, rolled up in their dirty fingers. And Stella looked down at them from the top step of her RV, her blonde hair backlit, her pale eyes invisible in that light but watching them, all of them. This was no longer even about sex or money, the twin udders of the world. This was something far more precious and mysterious, she thought, and so vast it made her feel insignificant. And yet it was through her that it was happening. Stella resisted the urge to close the door, to let these men rot in the hell of their own bodies. What was required of her now was something more than courage. It was a sort of heroism.

What else could she do but take each of them, in their pain and suffering, and love them?

Stella pointed to a hunchback at the end of the line, and the others moved aside as he slouched toward her.

II

GOD'S MADMEN

5

The room was dark, the windows distant. An immense room for small men. Such vast interiors were designed to remind their inhabitants that they did not amount to much, even if (as in this case) they were powerful, ambitious people. But the actual effect was the exact opposite: the high ceilings, the stucco, the gilding, the ancient carpets, the marquetry furniture, the Raphael frescoes... all this merely emphasized their dominance.

God was with them.

But they knew He was an ally who must be handled cautiously.

A sharpened blade. A double-edged blade.

There were four men. (Traditionally, tragedy works better with an odd number, but that's not the case here, so we'll just have to do our best.) In order of importance: the one dressed in white, in his organic cotton cassock perfectly suited to the sultry Roman summer, was Pope Rodolphe Krüger, aka Simon II. To his right, his secretary and (literally and metaphorically) his right-hand man, Otto Mühl. The others seated at the oval table were Cardinal Gordini, dean of the College of Cardinals, and Cardinal Carter, representing his thirteen American counterparts. For the record, the language they spoke was not English but Latin. More elegant, right?

They broke their fast on tea and coffee, on *ciambelle* and cream cakes. Their robes ended up covered with crumbs, which were less noticeable on the papal white than on the cardinals' scarlet. They wiped the corners of their lips, burped discreetly with a hand over their mouths.

Otto Mühl, dressed in a black jacket and a dog collar, was impeccable, having consumed nothing but a black coffee; no sugar, no milk, nothing. (He'd had a gastroscopy recently, and that had been impeccable too: no cancer, not a single polyp, nothing.) The others were waiting to hear what he had to say.

Jeremy Carter had traveled four thousand miles by airplane to tell them what was happening in his own country. His fingers drummed lightly on the varnished oak table. No prior communication had been permitted, whether by telephone, email, or Zoom. It was a subject of such seriousness that it required one's physical presence and could be discussed only orally. And not one word spoken in this room would leave these walls unless His Holiness decided otherwise.

"You seem impatient, Carter," said Gordini.

"This is big!" Carter said. "But I'll let His Holiness's secretary fill you in on the details."

"So what are we waiting for?" demanded the pope. "*Disputatio*, Otto!"

Otto cleared his throat. He had the kind of small, weaselly face suited to constant throat-clearing. Finally he spoke.

"The information was passed on to us by a certain Father Brown, from the parish of Jesup in the state of Georgia, in the United States of America. According to a confession heard less than seventy-two hours ago, a man was cured of his psoriasis by a certain Stella Thibodeaux —"

"This Father Brown... is he reliable?" Cardinal Gordini interjected.

"Absolutely," the secretary replied. "He's a former soldier, and we have no doubts whatsoever about his sense of duty."

"It's true—there's nothing better than a converted sinner."

"*Persevera*, Otto," urged the pope.

"Yes. Well, I, um... So, according to Father Brown, this girl also helped a man recover the use of his paralyzed arm, and —"

"Really?" the pope asked.

"And, uh, another man was cured of chronic leukemia —"

"*Miraculum!*" exclaimed Simon II.

"*Sine ullo dubio,*" added Gordini.

"*Gratias ago Deo.* Thank you, Lord, we needed this... How long have we been waiting for a manifestation of the Almighty?" Simon II asked. "This is excellent news, don't you think, Carter? And in your own beautiful homeland too!"

"Like I said, this is big," Carter replied.

"If we can verify the three miracles, we'll have a saint— a living saint!" Gordini said excitedly. "Canonization, and *santa subito!*"

"We don't have any American saints," Simon II observed. "Yes, this is perfect, wonderful! What a day! Otto, pass me another one of those delicious cakes."

"His Holiness is supposed to be watching his cholesterol," the secretary reminded him.

"To hell with it—give me two, Otto!"

Gordini crossed himself. "And how old is this woman?"

"Nineteen," replied Otto, passing the small bowl of *ciambelle* to the pope. "However, I... I'm afraid there's something I must add which may, um, dampen your enthusiasm."

"And what is that?" Carter demanded.

"This girl... I made a few inquiries about her, and, uh..."

"Ah," said Carter.

"Yes?" Gordini prompted.

"She is... how can I put this? She's a *meretrix mulier*."

"Why is that a problem, Otto?" Gordini asked. "Mary Magdalene is our most famous whore. And we are living in the age of inclusion, aren't we? In fact, it's been our credo for more than two thousand years: inclusivism! *Restauratio unitatis...*"

"Yes, but... I... I'm trying to find the most delicate way of explaining this to you... This girl performs her miracles by way of her, um... her most intimate bodily parts. That is to say, she —"

"You mean her pussy?" Carter said.

"Oh!" exclaimed Simon II.

"Precisely," Otto said. "She eases men's suffering with her... her *vagina*."

"Are you saying one must sleep with her in order to be cured?" Gordini asked.

"Yes."

"And that's the only way she —"

"*Prorsum,*" the secretary replied, nodding.

And there, in that large room where small men wielded great power, the carefree Roman summer so often eulogized by Catullus was chilled by a frosty silence.

"Yes, I see," said Simon II, nervously dusting crumbs from his lap with his sausage fingers. "In that case, we have a serious problem."

"What else do we know about this prostitute?" Carter asked.

The secretary barely looked up from the sheet of paper in front of him. "Abandoned at birth. Nineteen years old.

28

Blonde. No more than an elementary education. Lives in and works out of a recreational vehicle, so she has no fixed abode."

"Which means she has no family, and probably not many friends. No roots to speak of. That's good for us."

"In what way?"

"A living saint is impossible under such circumstances, I think we can all agree on that," Carter said. "But a martyr… Martyrdom would enable us to erase and transcend this girl's past, irrespective of her profession and her condition."

"Cardinal, surely you're not suggesting we —"

"Don't say another word, Otto!" Simon II interrupted.

"Well, this does concern your territory," Gordini said to Carter.

The American nodded. "And we are each expected to look after own affairs, I know."

"I know nothing about this, Carter, you understand? Nevertheless, you have carte blanche when it comes to this case. You're right—a saint-turned-martyr is an excellent idea. Afterward, we can create a past for the girl. Carter, make sure it's spectacular, horrible… and viral. I want half of the planet's inhabitants to witness Stella Thibodeaux's final moments on their smartphones."

"You can depend on me, Your Holiness. We're the best when it comes to this sort of thing."

"Absolutely. On the appointed day. *Vade in pace*, my friends," concluded the pope. "And bring me some seltzer water, Otto. I am suffering with heartburn. It is the price one pays for being too sensitive."

6

On the other side of the ocean, in the hot and troubled Georgian night (because there's a time and a place for turmoil and torment), Stella took out her notebook and wrote down a few details about her most recent clients. Her sentences were simple and short, like a schoolgirl's, and when she wasn't sure of the spelling of a certain word she would look it up in her old dictionary. She didn't fully understand why she did this, but it was an exercise she had performed since her earliest days as a prostitute. A way of commemorating these details of her life, and all these bodies, which tended to blur into one in her memory, a mass of flesh returning to the anonymity of the multitude. Sometimes she would remember an act of violence or an expression of shame, occasionally a tender gesture. She would remember their declarations of love too. But each time what truly remained, what would always remain, was the sadness, the sense of failure and loneliness. Because two bodies merging like that was never nothing, never insignificant, no matter what anyone says or thinks.

So Stella noted down a few lines about each of them. When she'd finished, she felt calmer, almost reassured. Besides, she couldn't bother Santa every night with her worries.

She took a cold beer from the icebox, then sat outside her motor home. Alone and steeped in melancholy, she smoked a cigarette and gazed up at the stars until her neck started to ache. The warm humidity made her skin tingle. The breeze carried scents of sage and eucalyptus. No matter how long Stella stared at the sky, she couldn't imagine a future beyond the next day.

Stella had saved her description of the hunchback until last, even though he'd been her first client of the day. About him, she had noted simply: *resorption.*

She had misspelled it at first. But then she'd checked the word in her dictionary.

7

The chauffeur hurried to open the door for him, before putting the cardinal's wheeled suitcase in the trunk and sitting behind the wheel, on the other side of a Plexiglas divider. His Eminence Jeremy Carter had flown business class on American Airlines and was now in the back seat of a stretch limousine with smoked windows.

The Cadillac moved away as if floating over the ground, imposing its dark mass in the flow of traffic, sure of its own importance. Beside the cardinal, Brenda Moore—her endless legs sheathed in silk stockings, her magnificent chest bulging from a fitted dark-blue power suit, luxuriant black hair, long-lashed green eyes, bee-stung lips... you get the idea—opened the limousine's minibar and poured a glass of neat whiskey. She handed it to the cardinal, who thanked her with a nod, pleased she had anticipated his desire. Carter took off his scarlet skullcap, revealing a bald spot. Brenda fixed a menthol cigarette to her silver holder, lit it, and blew a translucent cloud of smoke across the car's interior. How many men would not gladly have taken His Eminence's place at that very instant?

"Good trip?" Brenda asked, sounding a little bored at her own rhetorical question.

"Excellent. The menu has improved markedly since we told them it was unacceptable."

"I can tell. You've put on weight, Carter."

"When I was a bishop, I still had time to work out. But since becoming a cardinal... No, you're right. I need to get fit again. The trouble is, when you wear robes like these, it's easy to hide the extra pounds. The bagginess is ideal for expansion... Anyway, my dear, what else is on your mind?"

Brenda took a drag on her cigarette while Jimmy sipped his whiskey.

"Carter, are you sure you're doing the right thing where this young woman is concerned?"

"Are you questioning our information? We have the best intelligence network in the world, my dear: the confessional. It's like the respiratory system, you see. There are the pulmonary alveoli, then the bronchioles that lead to the bronchi, which are in turn connected to the —"

"I get it, Carter. I did go to school, you know. I just mean, it's always regrettable to get rid of a pretty girl. It's kind of a waste."

"Beauty is infinite, Brenda. And it is everywhere, and it renews itself in ways we cannot even imagine. Other beautiful women will come and take her place. You are the living proof of that."

"Thank you, Carter. But please remember I will never sleep with you."

"So the robes don't tempt you? You aren't eager to see what's underneath?"

"When you were talking about expansion, did you also mean that part of your anatomy?"

"Naturally."

"Well, I'm not completely incurious, but don't forget I'm a woman of power. I'm not sexually attracted to men from that point of view. Or any other, for that matter. So?"

"So, returning to a strictly professional point of view, when do you think you'll deal with my problem?"

"I'm going to put the Bronski brothers on the case, but —"

"The Bronski brothers! Really?"

"… but they're otherwise engaged at the moment."

"You're not pulling any punches!"

"If you want a good martyr, they're your guys. So, let's say… in three or four days? A week at the most."

"Well, I wish we could get it over with sooner…"

"Where can she go? It's a small world. A cruel one, too."

"Do as you think best. I trust you, Brenda. You'll receive my instructions and the target's coordinates tomorrow morning."

"The price will be higher than usual. I've had to delay two other contracts to fit you in."

"Money is no object."

"So you're breaking the piggy bank for this one…"

"Hardly, my dear."

"Well, I think you've reached your destination, Your Eminence."

As Brenda spoke, the magnificent, illuminated dome of the Capitol appeared in the American night. Inside lay miles of corridors, offices, security checks, a veritable anthill of power that led to an oval office in a nearby building. The meeting in Rome, Carter said, had not been solely about little Stella Thibodeaux; there was also the question of a diplomatic suitcase to be delivered from the Vatican to the White House.

In God We Trust.

"Do you know what's in it?" Brenda asked.

"No idea. But just between us, I'd prefer not to know. And so would you, believe me. *Simplex et rectum est in anima videt quod nihil mali passus est.* The simple, good soul sees evil nowhere."

"*Vade in pace*, Carter."

8

The ripple effect. Stella knew the expression, of course. But your understanding of phrases changes when you experience them for yourself. This is what determines the density of a human life. This is what makes you listen more attentively to the advice you are given.

The ripple effect.

There were at least fifty of them waiting outside her motor home. Stella had gone off to grab a hot dog and a Sprite at one of the carnival's food stalls, and now they had multiplied. They stood there in silence, resigned to waiting for as long as it took.

Stella hid behind a trailer and spied on them while she chewed her mustard-slathered hot dog. She was hungry. There had been five *resorptions* now. The last one had been a mute who'd run naked out of the RV, yelling at the top of his voice. It didn't work every time, though, naturally. And some of the men in that crowd had probably just come for a good fuck—thank God. But for the desperate ones seeking a cure, it required a sort of sincerity for it to work. When Stella plumbed the depths of their meager souls, stripped of all power and pride, she needed to find some core of goodness at their base. A pure feeling that had, for most of them, been destroyed by the harsh grind of poverty and suffering. Stella's compassion, what the churchmen's books call "loving thy neighbor," did the rest.

She retraced her steps and melted into the crowds strolling around the carousels, waiting until Santa Muerte had finished with her latest client. A young man emerged in tears from the trailer and Stella dove inside, breathing the mingled odors of sweat and patchouli oil he'd left behind.

"Are you making them cry now, Santa?"

"You know why they come, *querida*? For love and money. They all want to be happy and rich. I can bullshit them about wealth no problem, but when it comes to love... For God's sake, don't they know existence is nothing but a series of abandonments and a feeling of deep loneliness? Can't they see that? So what am I supposed to do about it? Some others seek glory, and they think that —"

"Santa, listen! Listen to me... There are, like, fifty of them waiting to see me now. I'm not looking for love or wealth or glory, I just want you to tell me what I should do."

"*Madre de Dios!* Fifty?"

Stella nodded.

Santa Muerte spat in her bowl, then said: "You could wait for us at the next stop."

"Are you going to the coast?"

"In three days."

"Works for me."

"Do you have enough cash?"

"I've got my savings."

"Good. Whatever you do, don't work, okay? Just put your feet up. Wait for them to forget about you..."

"Sure, Santa. I'll walk on the beach and smoke cigarettes. Like I'm on vacation."

"Exactly."

"What about the RV?"

"Just get in, start the engine, and drive away. Simple as that."

"But what if they follow me?"

"Leave tonight, but tell them you'll be back at work tomorrow morning. I can help if you want."

Stella walked over to the old woman, who smelled of mothballs and sweat, and kissed her on the forehead. "You're my only family, Santa, you know that?"

"I know, kid, I know. But sometimes, to survive, you need to leave your family behind."

9

For the small section of humanity that had ever had dealings with them, the Bronski brothers were a kind of plague. In fact, it was possible to put a number to the lives they had snuffed out since first founding their little company twenty-four years ago (next year was their silver jubilee). We owe this exactitude to the younger brother, William (Billy) Bronski, who had kept a running tally of the dead: 1,239 souls. About fifty per year, or a little less than one a week.

In other words, the two brothers were very hardworking. And given that now, in their early forties, they were reaching their peak, one could plausibly suggest that their output was likely to increase in the coming years, and that a large number of people would continue to shit their pants when they found out the killer siblings were after them.

"Huh? I can't hear you! What did you say?" yelled Michael (Mike) over the strident whine of the electric saw.

"We're out of thirty-gallon bags…"

"What?"

Mike finished slicing off the corpse's forearm, removed his finger from the trigger of the Bosch Saber Saw, and lifted up one side of his noise-canceling headphones.

"What were you saying, Billy?"

Billy picked up the severed forearm by the wrist, shook off the blood clots, and tossed it in the trash bag. "I was just saying we're out of thirty-gallon bags. All we've got left are tens."

"Okay. I'd better cut him into smaller pieces then."

"Sorry. I totally forgot about the bags. I know you don't like small pieces."

"It's okay. Everyone forgets stuff sometimes. I'm on my last legs too." He laughed at this. "So to speak."

The guy they were cutting up in the basement of a rental house had given them two sleepless nights. Billy and Mike needed to relax, to drink a nice cold beer and watch cars race around a track on a screen hung above the bar. As you might guess, the case that had brought the Bronski brothers to the glamorous environs of Beverly Hills involved a Famous Movie Star paid millions every year by a Multinational Corporation to be the face of their disposable coffee pods. Now, said Famous Movie Star was having a secret homosexual relationship with a Young Male Model. But this relationship had to end for the sake of the sales of the disposable pods. Unfortunately, the Young Male Model was threatening to spill the beans on the relationship if the Famous Movie Star dumped him. So the Multinational Corporation had called Brenda Moore, who had given the job to the Bronskis. One important clause in the contact stipulated that the Famous Movie Star would spend the final seventy-two hours in the company of the Young Male Model for one last wild bout of lovemaking (with the consent of the model himself, of course). Fearing that the Famous Movie Star might change his mind at the last minute for sentimental reasons, the Bronskis, like a pair of ticks, embedded themselves in the life of their target and held on tight. At dawn on the third day, the Famous Movie Star told his lover that he'd forgotten his cell phone in the hotel room and left the Young Male Model in the limousine to wait for him. But it was Michael Bronski who sat next to the young man, while William, the "chauffeur," was already behind the wheel, ready to drive the target to the rental house.

William also reported to his brother this final conversation between the two men:

FAMOUS MOVIE STAR
(with tears in his eyes)

You're the best, Valentino.
You, more than anyone, are
deeply buried within my soul.

YOUNG MALE MODEL
The one in your ass?

The Famous Movie Star then kissed his lover on the mouth, like Judas had done to Christ, before leaving the limousine as the credits rolled.

In the Bronski brothers' personal classification system, showbiz stars came second on the list of most annoying clients. In first place were politicians, who were difficult to eliminate due to the bodyguards that permanently surrounded them and also always begged the assassins to spare their lives until their very last breath. When confronted with pain and death, they were generally willing to promise absolutely anything, just as in their election manifestos.

Now they just had to finish chopping up this faggot before feeding him to the jackals in the desert.

Yeah, life's a bitch.

10

Everything went fine.

True, Santa had to intervene to get the men to leave her alone, but in the end Stella was able to get away just after eleven.

Now she was on US 341, headed for Jekyll Island. Stella liked driving at night. She savored the intimacy of being alone. And she always loved leaving one place to find another. Even if the reality often disappointed her, the possibility of being able to start over made her want to smile. She felt sure there must, eventually, be someone or something waiting for her. Meaning is a quest. And in that sense, Stella was about to get lucky.

In the cool damp night, with the dashboard glowing green and the moon hanging like an open parenthesis in the storm-cleansed sky, she lit a cigarette and blew smoke through the open window. She didn't need the radio for company. The caress of the wind and the hum of the engine were enough. It was exhausting to keep giving and giving. And now she'd discovered that her gift was something far greater than her body, she felt as if she was prematurely aging in her soul.

Like she was crumpling inside.

But anyway. The peaceful night would not go on forever. An external element was about to disrupt Stella's meditative introspection. For it is a rare and difficult thing to contemplate one's existence. In truth, Stella was tired of stories. She would have liked the narrative of her life to stop for a while, but the disruptive element was standing by the roadside, thumb raised.

She drove past the hitchhiker. The headlights' beam had revealed two things. No, three: loneliness, poverty, and beauty.

All of this was expressed in the physiognomy of the young man by the roadside as he turned on his heel, blinking in the glare and waving his arm.

Stella Thibodeaux and her damn empathy! She ought to think about herself, not others. Instead of which, she stepped on the brake and pulled onto the shoulder. An eighteen-wheeler screamed past, horn blaring. Silence fell in its wake as the young man appeared in her rearview mirror.

The passenger door opened with a creak. The young man climbed in beside her and smiled. He smelled of dust and diesel. His hair was long and blond, like Christ in those paintings you find in churches.

But Stella didn't notice the evil gleam in his eyes.

11

Time to suspend your disbelief.

Because other tragedies were occurring at the same time.

Life is a vale of tears, right?

Robert Smith could testify to that as he knelt weeping into his wife's lap.

This was the price to pay for his new face.

"So you went to see her, did you? You went to see that miracle chick!"

Even though they were together in the conjugal bedroom, Mrs. Smith did not stroke her husband's hair or offer any words of consolation. She was consumed by jealousy and bitterness, as if Stella's hands, by touching her husband's body, had stolen something from her. Her pride was wounded, and love is only love. Forgiveness would first require a desire to understand, but Mrs. Smith saw this as a chance to get rid of her cheating husband with an acrimonious (not to mention alimonious) divorce. Bob's small and peaceful life, the meager pleasures of an unambitious man, the faithful husband and attentive father, the law-abiding citizen and consumer... all of this collided with an intransigent Lutheran pragmatism.

"Just go back to your whore!" she said.

"She saved me," he replied pleadingly. "It's not like I betrayed you —"

"No? So you didn't stick your thing in her, then? That's not how she cured you? You're scum, Robert! You disgust me."

Robert felt more alone than he had ever felt in his life. What oppressed him was not loneliness itself, but loneliness in the presence of his wife: the worst kind of loneliness. But how could he explain the truth to someone who didn't want to understand?

The truth: that fate had put this girl in his path.

That he, Robert Smith, had—for once in his life—looked in the right place.

And seen.

The girl getting out of her chair and stretching in the radiant morning sunlight.

Her supple body promising sensual pleasures and Nietzschean laughter.

The backs of her thighs marked by the imprint of the chair's plastic straps.

Yes, he'd known then.

He'd felt his dick go hard and his whole future crystallize.

He'd known Stella Thibodeaux represented his one and only chance of redemption in the face of bitter duty, in the face of an existence founded on self-delusion.

His wife slapped him.

He bit his lip. Violence, at last. His defeated smile revealed teeth stained with blood.

Robert Smith and his wife would not grow old together.

12

At that precise moment, Stella was not a vision of possible happiness.

She was scared.

The young Christ was holding a switchblade under her chin, its point touching the fragile triangle of skin beneath her jaw. His other dirty hand had a strong grip on her hair and was pulling her head back. Stella did her best to swerve around the potholes that littered the empty Walmart parking lot, where the guy had told her to drive.

Her carotid artery pulsed against the sharpened steel.

She could easily have been killed, inadvertently, by a single jolt of the motor home on the pockmarked concrete. Life is stupid.

"Please put down your knife," said Stella. "I'll give you what you want. That's what I do for a living. My job is to give men exactly what you're looking for."

The hitchhiker turned to look behind him at the RV's bunk bed. He let go of Stella and began frantically rubbing his eyes.

"Where should I park?" asked Stella.

The man, bewildered, made a vague signal with his hand.

"Sir? Are you okay?"

The young man dropped his knife and put his head in his hands.

"I can't see! I can't fucking see anymore! What the fuck did you do to me, bitch?"

Stella stopped in the middle of the parking lot and engaged the brake. She opened the door and jumped out of the motor home. She could see lines of stacked supermarket carts, plastic bags fluttering in gusts of warm wind. The lampposts illuminated the white lines of the parking spaces, like an attempt to marshal chaos.

The guy kept screaming. As he tried to get out of the motor home, he banged his forehead against the door frame. Then he missed the step and fell face down on the heat-fissured asphalt.

"You fucking whore! Where are you? I'm gonna kill you!"

But he was no longer holding his knife. All he possessed now was his terror and the endless black nothingness that populated his night. He fell to his knees and started crying, begging her to do something.

Stella moved hesitantly toward the man. Then she ceased to hesitate. She walked up and touched him, her hand softly caressing his eyelids.

The young Christ looked up and became himself again, seeing Stella as she stood in the pale electric light of a lamppost: her long legs emerging from denim shorts, her feet bare in flip-flops, her breasts hanging loose beneath her tank top.

He stood, shaky with fear. Staggering backward, he hissed: "You... you're a witch. A witch..."

Then the guy started to run and disappeared around the corner of the supermarket. And in the words of the fable of the dog and the wolf, he took to his heels and is running yet.

Stella stood alone in the parking lot.

And so it was that the hope of a new beginning in a new place, that moment of intimacy in the light of the moon, in the green glow of the motor home's dashboard... all of that had been destroyed in an instant. It had all been so fragile. And Stella, in her innocence, did not even blame her attacker. She should have blamed him, of course. But, when she was born, Stella Thibodeaux was not given the option of anger.

She sat on the step of her RV and wept, wondering when all this would end. No matter how hard she looked, she couldn't find any way out of her situation. This was her life: a poor, abused orphan leading a miserable existence, but one recorded on the two pages of a social worker's report, without the lyricism of *Les Misérables*. She had felt estranged from her body as soon as men began staring at it, wanting to possess it.

And now, she had this... this gift.

But was it truly a gift? Or was it a curse?

The only way she had found not to belong to another person was to give herself to everybody.

Stella looked up at the stars and asked: "Why me?"

She remembered being a small child, in the care of nuns. The terror of seeing an apparition that would force her into grace.

"Why me?"

Have you noticed? The most important questions never get answered.

ZOOLOGIES

13

Billy Bronski scuffed the sole of his Tony Lama on the ground, raising a small cloud of dust. The crocodile-skin boots had been turned almost white by the effects of time and repeated bleach washes. Mike kicked a stone with his boa constrictor-skin boots, their scales worn as thin as his patience. The stone hit the patched-up fence surrounding the esplanade, and the worm-eaten wood made a hollow clunk. In places, under the burning sun, a few stunted tufts of grass suicidally peeked through the earth. Lethargy and desolation reigned here in the outskirts of the town of Jesup, where the carnival had set up camp for three weeks, briefly brightening the nights of the inhabitants with their blackened fingernails and baleful looks.

"They've fucked off," Mike observed.

"Yup, those assholes have gone alright."

"We're gonna have to question the locals to find out where they went."

"Right as always, brother."

Mike and Billy didn't need to lengthen this conversation to agree that they needed a cold beer in the closest bar. There was nothing better to help a man think. It was their way of mixing business with pleasure.

They found a bar just after the Chevron gas station. Getting out of their '69 Camaro, they slammed the doors shut behind them and pulled their jeans up to their navels. Mike stopped to readjust his balls, which had gotten trapped in the seam of his boxer shorts, then followed his brother. The fringes of their suede jackets stirred slightly in the breeze like a bunch of brown centipede legs as they swaggered forward, slaloming between the parked Harley-Davidsons. Now, we should bear in mind that—especially when they were thirsty and trying to enter a bar, but also in life generally—the Bronski brothers preferred to move in a straight line. Mike expressed his annoyance by spitting a gob of phlegm at a white Dunlop tire.

Billy pushed open the door, and the refrigerated air slapped him in the lungs. Behind him, Mike coughed.

At the back of the room, a dozen bikers froze around the pool table. Bikers are like children: instinctively curious but easily absorbed by their games. By the time the newcomers had taken a seat, the bikers were playing pool again.

When Frankie the bartender stood up after putting away a crate of empty bottles, he saw two broad-shouldered men sitting at the bar, Stetsons in front of them, a red band across each of their foreheads. He also saw two expressionless faces, reshaped by scalpels and collagen. Frankie wasn't to know this, but the Bronski brothers had been forced to change their identities and their faces so many times that they barely resembled human beings at all anymore; it was hard to imagine a mother producing two monsters like these. Frankie had seen his fair share of smashed-up faces, but something about these two told him to proceed with caution: to keep a safe distance and observe them for a while.

They ordered Schlitz beers. Three each.

Frankie arranged the six cans on the counter. The first to quench their thirst, the second to quench their thirst, the third to quench their thirst. After downing the last beer, both men crumpled the cans in their enormous hands before sliding the flattened aluminum disks back toward the bartender. "Takes up less space in your recycling bins," said Billy.

Frankie picked up the metal circles and tossed them into the trash can at his feet. "I don't have a recycling bin. Just regular garbage."

The bartender wiped the counter with a dish towel. Frankie Malone was not the kind of man to run away from adversity.

"Another beer?" Mike suggested to his brother.

"Good idea," said Billy. "I could do with a beer."

"Two beers," Mike called out.

Frankie returned with two cans of Schlitz, which he placed in front of his strange-looking customers. "On the house. Buy three, get one free."

"Nice. How long you been doing that?"

"Started today."

The Bronski brothers shared a glance. "Is our barman a comedian?" said Mike.

"Hey, when Frankie Malone buys you a beer, the least you can do is say thank you," said the former boxer. "If you're looking for trouble, on the other hand, I'm your man."

Mike and Billy stared at this tough-guy bartender, then looked at each other.

"Respect, man. You've got guts, I'll say that for you."

"Yup. Thank you, Frankie. From the bottom of my heart."

"No problem, guys. Drink your beer in peace and love."

"Hang on, buddy. We've got an unanswered question that might prevent us from drinking this beer in a neighbor-loving way…"

"See, what we want to know is this," said Mike. "Where did all those carnival folks go?"

"The carnies? What do you want with them?"

"That's our business," said Billy.

"Where'd they go?" Mike repeated.

"Toward the coast."

"You want to be a little more precise?"

"Southeast, I'd say."

"A little more precise than that?"

"No."

"Okay, we'll leave it there," said Mike, leaving a $10 bill on the bar. "At least we know which direction they're headed. Right, Billy?"

"We don't need much. Just the basics. We manage fine with just the basics. Thanks, buddy."

Mike and Billy stood up from their barstools. The cushions hissed as they rediscovered their normal shape, like an asthmatic who's been holding their breath too long. Frankie reckoned each man weighed between 220 and 240 pounds. Heavyweights. Ask a boxer to guess your weight and they'll rarely get it wrong.

The bell rang as Mike opened the door. The bikers paused their game to look up again, and Mike raised his hat to them. "See ya, bikers!" Billy laughed and followed his brother out the door.

The bikers stood stock still like those famous pillars of salt so abundant in literature. Outside, the two assassins got in their Camaro, which pulled away without the tires skidding on the gravel.

But Frankie's day wasn't over. From the corner of his eye, he saw a mountain of flesh growing bigger in his field of vision. The mountain of flesh in question walked slowly across the bar, 280 pounds of fat and muscle raised on Black Angus beef. Not even Frankie Malone wanted any trouble with this guy.

"Hey Frankie," the mountain said. "What did those two queers want?"

Frankie swallowed his spit, but he wasn't about to show his fear. "Normally I'd say it wasn't any of your business, but you're a good customer, so I'll tell you. They wanted to know where the carnies had gone."

"And?"

"I told them."

"Yeah? So where did those motherfuckers go?"

"Toward the coast."

"You weren't a little more precise?"

"Southeast, I said."

"More precise than that?"

"No."

"So they must have taken 341…"

"I reckon you're right."

The 280-pound mountain was nicknamed Comanche. A raised pink scar ran from his left cheek up to his forehead, where it disappeared under jet-black hair pulled back into a ponytail. Comanche was the leader of the local chapter of the Bandidos. In other words, he had already spent about fifteen years in prison for various acts of tomfoolery, including gang rape, meth dealing, and murdering someone with his bare hands.

A nice guy.

"Right now we don't have time to deal with this, because there's a guy here who owes us money. But if you ever see those queers again, will you let me know? I'd really appreciate it, Frankie, okay?"

Comanche took a grease-stained business card from the pocket of his Perfecto jacket and laid it on the counter. Yeah, I know, it seems a little strange. But believe me, Comanche was a businessman.

The giant snapped his fingers. In an instant his men downed their beers and put the pool sticks back in their rack. The Bandidos are not only curious and playful, but polite too, when they want to be.

There's just one thing you should know about them.

They don't like being called "bikers."

14

Night had fallen, bringing barely an iota of coolness to the hateful heat. The day shift of flies had gone home and the mosquitoes had taken their place. Anyone with a fan or an AC unit had it running full blast. It will come as no surprise that the only businesses in the area not suffering from the recession were those selling mosquito nets and air conditioners.

Oh, and Frankie Malone's bar.

Frankie asked Margot to tend bar for a while.

"Where are you going?" she asked.

"Shopping."

"Now?"

"That's why I'm asking you to look after my customers. No questions, Margot."

"Okay, Frankie."

Malone was carrying a large manila envelope, which he used to shoo away mosquitoes as he passed through a halo of light. Spiders as big as his thumb had spun their webs from every possible perch and were munching on all kinds of bugs. Natural selection was doing its thing. Mother Nature is a pitiless bitch.

Frankie didn't see many people as he walked—just some drunk youngsters driving beat-up pickups and the usual hobos lying on their cardboard mattresses in doorways. "A chicken in every pot, a car in every backyard," Herbert Hoover's election campaign had once promised. Of all the presidential slogans, that was maybe the most naive. Almost a century later, social evolution had brought us back, slowly and irreversibly, to its starting point: the descent into poverty. And in the rising tide of history, Frankie Malone was doing his best to keep his head above the waterline, dignified in defeat.

In his palm, the envelope's pale brown darkened with sweat. He switched it from hand to hand on a regular basis to keep the paper from turning to pulp. Truth was, he felt a little ashamed of the envelope's contents. He felt like a snitch, except that in this case it was pretty much an act of duty.

Fifteen minutes later, he passed the Taco Bell as it was closing and entered the church through the service entrance. He reached the vestry as Father Brown was taking off his stole and putting it on a hanger, having finished his last confession. The priest raised his large, gray-haired head and exclaimed, "Good grief, Malone! You need to learn to use the front door like everyone else!"

"I can't stand the idea of crossing myself, you know that. Seeing your Christ nailed to the cross gives me the creeps."

"It's simply an image to remind us that the best day was yesterday. A good confession's what you need, Malone. We can take our time and do it properly…"

"It's too late. I already lost my innocence, Jimmy."

("Jimmy" here is short for James. James Brown, like the singer. Father Brown was the subject of a whole bunch of lame jokes, as we will discover later.)

The priest unfastened his dog collar, took it off and placed it on his desk. He wiped sweat from the back of his neck with a wrinkled handkerchief, then mopped his brow. "Huh…" he said, looking at Malone.

"What?"

"You're bowlegged!"

"Yeah? So?"

"I never noticed that before."

Frankie shrugged. "Well, you only ever see me when I'm standing behind that damn bar. As far as my customers are concerned, I'm just a human torso."

"Exactly. So why didn't you wait for me to come and drink my beer instead of going out in this heat?"

"Two guys came to see me, Jimmy."

"So?"

"They were looking for the carnival people. Wanted to know where they'd gone. I told them they'd headed to the coast. I mean, I had to give them something, you understand? But I didn't tell them exactly where they'd gone."

"We must bring our own light to the darkness. Nobody is going to do it for us," the priest proclaimed ironically.

"Who's that—your Christ?"

"Charles Bukowski. Light my lantern, Malone…"

Time sped up. Father Brown took a flask from the inside pocket of his jacket and swallowed a mouthful before handing it to Frankie. In a crisis, we sometimes give in to temptation.

"Haven't touched a drop since 1984. I lost my title because of that shit."

"Okay. So… these two guys?"

"Well, I don't think they were after the carnies."

"No?"

"No."

"Who, then?"

"They were after that girl who follows the carnival. The one in the motor home. The blonde."

"You mean Stella? Stella Thibodeaux?"

"The miracle chick, yeah."

Father Brown shivered. He hated involuntary physical responses and drank another mouthful to regain his composure. He wished he could pretend there was nothing wrong, remain in the conditional past tense, the one that enables you to keep things at a distance, but that wasn't possible. Because the present overtakes everything, and then time speeds up.

"What makes you say that?" he asked disingenuously. "Maybe those guys had a problem with the carnival folks. Like, they owed them money or something…"

"No, Jimmy. Their faces. Their eyes… Call it my intuition if you like. They were bad guys. I've seen their type before. You weren't there, but I was… Do you still have your video recorder? Take a look at this."

With that, Frankie Malone finally took the shameful object out of the manila envelope: a video cassette recorded by a surveillance camera.

"Don't ask me why I've got this in my bar, Jimmy. Whatever you do, don't ask. But it's because of my insurance. If it wasn't for this, those bastards wouldn't renew my policy."

The priest reached out to grab the cassette.

Fuck, Jimmy, your hand's shaking.

On.

Play.

Images appeared on the screen. Black-and-white. Silent. Which only made them more terrifying. The door of the bar opened. The two guys sat on their stools. Despite the grainy picture, the faces of the Bronski brothers were clearly visible, smiling expressionlessly, mutely asking for six beers…

"Oh God!" gasped Father Brown.

"Is it that bad?"

"I think I've made a terrible mistake, Malone. The mother of all terrible mistakes."

15

The mother of all terrible mistakes was this: informing the diocese about the possibility of miracles. Someone there must have told the Bishop of Baltimore, who must in turn have referred the matter to Cardinal Carter. Within a few hours, the news had reached the Vatican.

And now Father Brown was trying to drown himself in a bottle of gin. The honest purity of juniper, its ability to distort a reality that was biting him, sinking its teeth deep into his flesh. Whiskey brought peace. Gin was for war.

Sitting naked on the edge of the tub, he looked up at the bathroom mirror and saw a lost-looking man with his tail between his legs. Father Brown took another gulp of alcohol. He should have known: a prostitute could never be a saint. Compassion did not stretch that far. The Holy See had spent almost two thousand years setting out its myth. The Roman Catholic religion had become a state, with its own employees, its secret police, its intellectuals, its Swiss

Guard. It had its own banks, businessmen, investors, press, publishing house, and economy.

It was a multinational corporation in charge of more than one billion three hundred million people.

Not bad for a long-haired young man who'd died at thirty-three, dressed in a simple robe and leather sandals, armed with nothing but the spoken word.

And where the spoken word was concerned, it was true Father Brown would have been better off keeping his mouth shut. But he'd felt duty bound to pass on the information to his superiors. Blame the obsessive obedience of the Navy SEALs, which had led so many to their graves. And now, despite everything, his dick was hardening. Ever since he'd chosen abstinence, his body had been estranged from him, his balls as hard as rocks.

Father Brown got into the tub, turned on the shower, and aimed it at his erection. The cold water caused a loss of vigor below but an increase in lucidity up above.

Now.

Now, yes.

Now he owed a debt to that girl.

He had thought a part of his life would never return, that certain actions would never be repeated.

He'd thought kindness could replace cruelty.

He'd thought giving without expecting anything in return was The Way.

But that didn't account for the boomerang effect. Some people have a destiny they can never escape. A past that returns to haunt them.

Father Brown sat in the bathtub and directed the jet of ice water over his whole body. He gasped and panted, staying there until his skin had turned purple, while continuing to drink from the bottle of gin, his heart pumping the alcohol through his bloodstream even faster because of the cold. He knew all about that. He'd been trained to resist low temperatures.

Dripping, his muscles hardened, he opened the shower curtain and staggered toward his bedroom, where he opened the door of the wardrobe. Beneath its false bottom was a fake passport, a thousand dollars wrapped in a rubber band, a stick of C-4 explosive, two burner phones, a Mossberg 500, and a SIG Sauer P220. The bullets were hidden in another location.

The emergency arsenal of a man with a murky past and an uncertain future.

Brown pumped the breech of the shotgun.

Naked as the day he was born.

Till death do us part, Stella Thibodeaux.

16

Santa Muerte had earned her name—Saint Death—because she loved life, because you couldn't have one without the other. As a young woman, she had known men: the sensations provided by their bodies, their words, their hands, their promises, some kept and some not, like dreams that came true or taunted you with their unreality. She had known desires, fulfilled and frustrated, and journeys, and pleasures, and now and then the relief of a comfortable existence. But what you need to remember is that she had known love. And unlike most of us, whose passions fade into the past, leaving us with pangs of sadness and regret, cowards that we are, the man she loved was still sleeping beside her, as he had every night since their first encounter thirty-odd years earlier, on Solana Beach.

The love of Santa Muerte's life, discovered in the autumn of her years, was a man named Tarzan.

Tarzan was ninety-two now, skinny and bald. When Santa and her lover embraced, you could hear their bones knocking together. Tarzan no longer had his loincloth or his muscles. He no longer swung across the upper reaches of the circus tent on his vine-like rope to rescue a young woman surrounded by tame lions pretending to want to eat her. Nowadays, Tarzan cleaned the animals' cages while they watched him indifferently. It is one of the privileges of old age that one no longer arouses any kind of appetite.

But Santa still remembered the Tarzan who used to pose on that Californian beach, lifting heavy weights, his oiled skin rippling with muscles. He had already been in his sixties back then. And she had been touched by his superficial refusal to surrender to the logic of time. Santa was a small, supple, slender woman, and Tarzan would sometimes be a little clumsy with her, squeezing her too tightly in his arms. When that happened, she would grimace with pain, but at the same time she loved his strength—his strength which was now nothing more than gentleness.

Old age is like a spring roll: the tender past wrapped inside the skin's crust. So, tonight, Santa slipped between her husband's arms, disturbing his sleep so she could nestle her head in the crook of his neck. Their trailer smelled of mold and stale cigarette smoke. Thanks to the effects of old age, there was no longer any need to replace the old curtains to hide their nudity from the waxing moon whose light blinded them in the warm darkness. Through the open window, she could hear the night breathing: the purr of an engine mingled with the rustling of sycamore leaves in the wind. And, in the distance, the soft roar of the ocean, the hiss of waves on sand. Tarzan had unhooked their trailer from the Ford pickup. The big top had been raised. The Mexican fortune teller's first clients had flocked to see her instantly, avid—as they were every year—for answers about their fate.

Turning her head slightly, Santa looked at the crystal ball on the round table. As always, she'd covered it with a cloth for the night. Who can tell where imposture ends and genuine belief begins? That morning, she had gone to see Stella, who had settled herself in a quiet area of a beach. They'd hugged, shared a whole pot of coffee and smoked cigarettes while Santa advised her to stay away from the fairground. As her head rose and fell in time with Tarzan's breathing, Santa sensed the halo of a vague foreboding. "My love…" she whispered.

Tarzan was wide awake in an instant. They had been robbed too many times over the years.

"It's okay," she said. "Calm down, it's only me…"

"You're more than enough for me, my wrinkled goddess."

"Ah, you've always been a poet in your own way, my shrunken hero."

"What's up, Santa?"

"It's just… We don't have any children, Tarzan."

"That's why you woke me? You want me to give you a child now?"

Santa pressed herself against him. Tarzan felt the shudder of her silent laughter, her sharp jaw sawing his ribs.

Tarzan sat up, grabbed the pack of Camels from the foot of the bed, and lit two cigarettes. The beam of moonlight was a steel blade across the trailer's threadbare carpet. He used the empty Dr Pepper can as an ashtray and said: "Tell me, Santa. What's bothering you?"

"Men will come. They're looking for the girl."

Tarzan had learned to take his wife's premonitions seriously. "Bad men?" he asked.

Santa nodded. "We need to protect her…"

"So we'll be her mother and father? Is that what you mean, Santa?"

"Are you ready?"

Tarzan drowned his cigarette stub in the puddle of soda at the bottom of the can, then slowly took off his nightshirt.

She had time to finish her smoke before he was ready. As she did so, she thought about something that had nothing to do with Stella or her worries about the present. She thought about how men always had to get it up for sex, and how glad she was that she didn't have to bear the onerous responsibility of that task herself, how she would much rather be a woman and welcome him in.

Santa lay on her back and spread her legs.

Crick-creak-crack

went their bones.

But it was good.

It was always good, however old they were.

17

They were the lethal, inescapable instruments of fate.

They didn't rush, because fate takes its time.

They'd slept in a roadside motel. In twin beds, the TV flickering silently all night long. Now, at dawn, Mike turned it off as he went to the bathroom. He and his brother had never been able to sleep without some source of light. The dark had always scared them, because they knew all the monsters it concealed.

Billy heard his brother pissing into the toilet bowl, followed by the sound of the flush. But there was nothing poetic about this pale blue morning. The Bronski brothers weren't Stella; they didn't embody grace. They were breakers, twisters, destroyers. As ruthless and soulless as fate itself.

Billy got up next. The pressure on his bladder gave him a hard-on that made a tent of his briefs. As he came back into the bedroom, Mike looked away, embarrassed. Ignoring this, Billy said: "It's your turn, Mike."

"I know, that's why I'm getting dressed."

"I didn't hear you brush your teeth."

"I'll do it later."

"Mom would be sad if she could see you."

"I said I'd do it later."

"Why change the habit of a lifetime?"

"Because habits can betray us. They find us, they watch us, and early one morning they put a bullet in the back of our head."

"We're not at war, Mike. Nobody's watching us."

"So you say."

"For fuck's sake! What's up with you this morning?"

Michael Bronski finished buttoning up his jeans, slid his Glock under the back of his belt, then covered it with his untucked Hawaiian shirt emblazoned with a parrot pattern. Next he put on his leather boots (no socks: a matter of principle for a free man). He lifted the corner of the curtain and glanced through the window at the courtyard, empty in the early-morning light. His brother watched as Mike unbolted the door and went outside.

Billy was raising the toilet lid when he heard the door open. He quickly grabbed the rifle hidden inside the bathtub, rushed to the corner of the room, and pumped the breech. Mike froze, one hand hovering over the nightstand. Billy lowered the barrel and exhaled.

"Jesus, Mike, what the hell are you doing?"

"I forgot the quarters."

Mike quietly shut the door behind him and headed over to the nearby vending machines. He bought two paper cups of black coffee from the first machine, and two cellophane-wrapped bacon-and-egg sandwiches from the second. Every other day, it was his turn to buy breakfast, and he kept a bunch of quarters for that reason: the quarters he'd just retrieved from the ashtray on the nightstand.

He looked down at the parking lot, where several vehicles were parked diagonally like dominoes on a flat surface. He thought about *Flatland*, a novel that takes place in a two-dimensional world. If he hadn't been a hitman, Michael Bronski would have chosen to be a writer. As long as you had creative potential, both jobs could be satisfying.

Beyond the parking lot, traffic sped by intermittently on the interstate. Mike went back to their room, a coffee in each hand, the sandwiches wedged in his armpits.

He heard a sort of clinking sound and knew instantly what it was. Sometimes a man can have a deep connection with his automobile, and that was the case with the Bronski brothers and their 1969 Chevrolet Camaro RS Coupé. Bottle green, with two white stripes running along the hood and the roof. A rare model. The Bronskis had always paid attention to their style, and there was a particular pleasure to be felt from the vibration of a V8 engine purring like a leopard.

Mike balanced the coffees and sandwiches on the edge of the railing, moved stealthily down the staircase, as silent and agile as that leopard he'd been thinking about, and ran across the parking lot to pistol-whip the car thief on the back of his head. Just a small cuff, enough to make a man puke with the pain. The skinny, long-haired man dropped the piece of wire he'd been holding and tried to break his fall by hanging onto the car's hood. Mike kicked his ankles away and, once the thief was lying face down on the ground, turned him over so he could see Mike's face and realize what a big fucking mistake he'd made by targeting this particular vehicle.

Mike liked to vary his pleasures. He pressed the barrel of his gun against the young man's forehead. He saw the blue irises grow larger and took in the uncanny resemblance to Christ, the emaciated look of a possible junkie.

"Please… don't kill me, I —"

"You'll need to beg better than that."

"I… I saw the ten-dollar bill on the seat… I wasn't after the car… Just the ten dollars… I don't even have a license…"

Mike's hand tightened around the boy's neck. "So you're going to die for the sake of ten dollars. Kind of dumb, don't you think?"

"I… I don't have any money… That girl's got my bag… It's in her motor home, you see, and I —"

Mike loosened his grip slightly.

The young Christ sensed the possibility of escape. "This girl… I was hitchhiking and she… she touched me and made me blind… and then she cured me…"

The hand let go of his neck.

"A blonde girl?" asked Mike.

The boy nodded.

"I'm guessing you tried to fuck her?"

The boy nodded again.

"And she made you blind?"

The boy nodded a third time.

"And then she gave you back your sight?"

The boy... well, you get the idea.

"And this girl... did she say where she was going?"

"She... she said something about Jekyll Island, I think..."

"What's your name?"

"Huh?"

"Tell me your fucking name, dickhead!"

"J—"

"Juh? That's your name?"

"J... J... Jason."

"Did anyone happen to mention that today's your lucky day, Jason?"

"N... No."

"Well, it is. Get up. You're going to tell my brother everything you said to me. Everything, you hear me?"

"You... You have a brother?"

Mike smiled. "Yeah, when they see us, people usually say something lame like 'trouble comes in twos.' Move your ass, Jason—my coffee's going cold."

18

Stella sank her bare feet into the sand. She looked around, a little lost but fascinated, as the waves crashed on the shore and crept up to wet her toes. Stella couldn't swim. She hadn't read Stevenson either. In fact, she wasn't even aware he'd written *The Strange Case of Dr. Jekyll and Mr. Hyde*. Since she didn't know about the connection between that author and *Treasure Island*, she couldn't recognize the irony of finding herself on an island called Jekyll (even if the island was linked to the mainland by a bridge) which was still in a state of enchantingly beautiful wildness. Through years of yielding to men's bodies, she had forgotten the nature of the elements, the placid immensity of the sea, and the wonderfully soothing and liberating effects it could have on those who took the time to lose themselves in contemplation of it.

During the three years she'd worked as a prostitute, she had never imagined being able to do anything else. And this morning, Stella realized she hadn't touched a man's body in the last forty-eight hours. She felt better for it, even if she missed the habitual gestures of soaping a foreskin, caressing a pair of testicles, unrolling a condom. It was a job and she was its slave, the victim of a form of alienation she couldn't even name.

But here, in this perfect moment, as she breathed in the iodine-laced oxygen, as she felt the damp sand under her feet, her calf muscles tensing beneath her skin, the perfect movement of the ocean's fluid mechanics, the emotion of a detail, it was as if she'd found the place where God was hiding.

Speaking of which, there remained the problem of the grace bestowed upon her. Naively, Stella wished she could ask the trees, the birds, and the sea foam about this supernatural gift. But the trees, birds, and foam remained indifferent. She found herself in a body that made no sense. She possessed something others wanted, something whose essence she didn't even understand.

Stella stopped. She didn't know where to go, and she was alone, dressed in cutoffs and a T-shirt, her feet bare. She thought about Santa. She needed her comforting presence, right here, right now, but she had promised not to go see her anytime soon. She needed to wait, to stop using her gift. She was alone with her skin, her body, and her grace.

Alone.

Absolutely alone.

Until she saw that man crouching at the back of her motor home, which she'd parked on the edge of the beach, concealed by bushes. He was in the process of removing her license plate and replacing it with another one.

Stella picked up a shard of broken glass half-buried in the sand and went over to him.

"Hey, sir! What are you doing?"

The man paused. He had a gray brush cut and broad shoulders. Without turning to face her, he said: "I'm trying to save your life, Stella Thibodeaux."

IV

FREAKS

19

Meredith Watson stopped in the doorway of Luis Molina's office. She didn't need to do anything to get his attention: when Meredith came close, a sort of sixth sense made you look up. Her twisted, arthritic index finger beckoned the journalist to follow her. The editor of the *Savannah News* was five feet tall and had one leg shorter than the other, but this did not prevent her walking at a diabolical pace. *Ka-shlop ka-shlop ka-shlop.* Luis got seasick just from trying to keep up with her.

Luis closed the door of the frosted-glass box. Meredith went around her desk and climbed into her wheelchair, on which she had placed a cushion that enabled her to look her interlocutors in the eye. She picked up two sheets of paper from the mail basket and placed them on the desk blotter, alongside a Bic ballpoint pen, a notepad, and a telephone.

"What's all this, Molina?"

Meredith had the rasping voice of a smoker, a voice like gravel being poured into a plastic jug with a handle that was threatening to fall off but which you still kept using every day.

Now to Luis: a short, dark-skinned man from Honduras. He still had vague memories of the slums of Tegucigalpa before his father had carried him, aged six, across the Rio Grande and had entered the Promised Land. Orphaned and then fostered at ten, he'd been a diligent student who'd gone down the path of university education and American naturalization. He had recently married, and his wife was already pregnant. An exemplary resumé.

Except that Meredith Watson did not give a flying fuck about exemplary resumés. She wanted well-written, effective articles (and from this point of view, Luis was one of her best employees), but what she wanted more than anything were reliable sources.

"I don't see anything reliable here, Molina—and that's an understatement."

"It's a proposal to introduce the subject, to hook the readers in —"

"I know how this works, Molina. I'm guessing you heard this gossip in a bar?"

"Several bars. In several towns."

"Villages, you mean?"

"I… I heard this story when I went to write about that alligator at Point Creek, then at the fire in —"

"That's enough, Molina. I know what appears in my newspaper. Drunk men in bars talking about a goddamn saint, Molina… Do you know what this means?"

"I think so, yeah."

"No, you don't. It could mean a Pulitzer, Molina! If this story is true, the *Savannah News* could win a Pulitzer!"

"Give me a week to get to the bottom of this."

"I'll give you three days, Molina. I want first-person testimonies about the miracles, I want the events reconstructed. But, most importantly, I want you to find the girl. Interview, photo… get everything you can on her. And keep your receipts."

"Yes, ma'am."

"Fucking hell, Molina. Why did this have to happen to you?"

20

"I'm sorry, kid. I am so, so sorry."

Her hair disheveled, her cheeks bright red, her mouth gagged, her hands and feet duct-taped to the chair, Stella stared in shock at Father Brown. He'd had to use all his strength to overpower her while trying to avoid hurting her. Her hands were tied behind her back, pushing her breasts forward; her nipples dimpled the white T-shirt, which was now streaked with red. Father Brown used a dirty handkerchief to wipe the blood from his forehead and his nose, which were covered with painful pink scratches.

The motor home's walls muffled the sound of the sea. Albatrosses floated in the sky above, their vast wings outstretched, crying out under the roar of the wind. Sitting on a bench at right angles to the bunk, Father Brown carefully examined the girl. Stella was beautiful and fierce. Not beautiful in the way you think, but beautiful in the way you know: an undeniable beauty that hit you in the guts. Stella's eyes were the windows of a soul that spoke directly to yours. All it took was a single look and you were called, you were chosen. But you've heard all this already. Long story short: you were neck-deep in the shit known as bewitchment. Stella was a bit like a Gorgon, except her blonde hair smelled of lavender shampoo and Marlboro Lights, and instead of turning you to stone, looking into her eyes made you feel more alive. One look from Stella and you felt ten feet tall.

"Look at this dog collar, look at this crucifix pinned to my jacket," said Father Brown. "I'm a man of God, not a psychopath. I'm a priest—a real one. And if everything that's happened, everything that's about to happen to you, has put you in this uncomfortable situation... well, you should know it's all my fault."

Stella didn't move. She didn't look away from this strange man whose hands were stained with dried blood and dust. Her chest continued to rise and fall anxiously. Her little heart kept pumping hard. She was desperate to free herself, to live without fetters, to stop being duct-taped to a chair so tightly that she was getting pins and needles in her fingertips.

Father Brown picked up the pack of cigarettes and the ashtray from the foot of the bed. He was about to grab the lighter from inside the bed, but he changed his mind.

"But I swear to you that I'm the good guy in this story, no matter what you might think right now."

Silence.

"Okay, Stella, so do you think we can have a conversation without you going apeshit again? For example, could I untape your mouth without you screaming your head off? Could we have a calm discussion between two well-intentioned people?"

Stella didn't move.

"I'm going to smoke my cigarette outside. When I come back, I —"

Stella nodded.

"Are you sure?"

Stella nodded again. Father Brown retraced his steps and gently removed the duct tape from her mouth. Stella took a deep breath, coughed, then ran her tongue over her lips. "You can... smoke inside. I'm an occasional smoker myself..."

Father Brown raised a bottle of water to her lips and helped her to drink a few mouthfuls. She thanked him.

"Now untie me."

"Not till you've heard what I have to say."

"Please..."

"Listen to me, Stella. Two men are looking for you. I know these men, and when they're after you, it's never good news. And if I'm the good guy in this story, then they're definitely the bad guys. Really, seriously bad guys. In less than an hour, they'll probably be here. Exactly where I am now. They're like bloodhounds. They could find you if you were hiding in the devil's asshole. Do you understand?"

"A priest doesn't talk like that."

"Let's say I'm expressing a buried part of my nature. And that part is using colloquial language so you can fully appreciate the urgency of the situation."

"You don't have to use fancy words to explain things either."

"Okay. Listen, it's very simple. We're going to get out of here, fast. The first thing we need to do is put as many miles as we can between them and us."

"But why?"

"Why what?"

"Why are they looking for me?"

"Because it appears that you've performed miracles, Stella."

"*Resorptions*," Stella corrected him. "Santa calls them *resorptions*."

"Who's Santa?"

"She's like my mom. She and Tarzan are the only family I have."

"Tarzan?"

"He's her husband. Actually, no, he's more than that. He's the love of her life."

"For God's sake, Stella, who are these people?"

"They work at the carnival. Santa's a fortune teller. She can read palms and cards, and she has a crystal ball too... What, you don't believe me?"

"What I wanted to believe was that I lived in a world where faith supported reason. But I can see now that chaos reigns here. The entropy of chaos…"

"I don't understand. I mean, I don't really care—it's never bothered me, not understanding—but… But why do they want to hurt me if I'm… if I can perform miracles, as you put it?"

"Because… Because you're a prostitute."

"So?"

"So, apparently you cure these men by giving them pleasure. And that pleasure, when practiced outside the sanctity of marriage, is considered a sin."

"So?"

"So… I can only give you another answer you won't understand."

"Tell me anyway."

"Because of dogma."

"Ah."

"Dogma."

"Is that all?"

"A dogma is an indisputable truth. You're a sort of Virgin in reverse, Stella. You understand? Your simple existence calls into question two thousand years of history."

"Really? That's all?"

"That's enough for now. Okay, I'm going to untie you and get you out of here. Do I have your word?"

"You do. My wrists hurt, you know. Like, really bad… But hang on, how did you know I was here?"

"I used to be a bloodhound too."

"Hmm. So do you have a name, Mr. Bloodhound-Priest?"

"Brown."

"Brown what?"

"Um… James. James Brown."

"Like the soul singer? 'Sex Machine' and all that?"

"That's right."

"You know what James Brown used to say?"

"No, Stella. What did he say?"

"Turn on the heat and build some fire."

21

There wasn't much to it: a rectangular enclosure, about two and a half acres, with a few rides for kids and teenagers, and some stalls offering games, food, and drinks. There was a small circus tent where Tarzan led two lions on a leash to the yawning lion tamer, where a sad clown who smelled of beer and garlic fell and got up again, where three wiry trapezists supported each other, where the rubber-jointed contortionist unfolded and revealed herself as a fragment of the world. But there was also this: in the Hall of Miracles tent, you could see the Snakeskin Woman, the Man With Elephant Balls, the Siamese Brothers who shared a single brain (did they dream the same dreams, like the same foods, yearn to escape each other?), the Albino Dwarf you could pick up and cuddle, the Human Torso who walked on his hands, the Fork-Tongued Turk who could roll two cigarettes at once. And then there was the heartbroken Weeping Man, who could cry you a river at the drop of a hat, twin furrows dug deep in his cheeks by the tracks of his tears, a man whose grief was as vast as a lake of pure pain. And finally there was Santa Muerte and her crystal ball, the seer who in reality did not read the future in palms or cards but in the cracks of wrinkled faces, in the sadness of eyes. In the suffering of others, Santa saw the hope that would soothe it.

There wasn't much to it, but it was enough to entertain the inhabitants of Fernandina Beach on a Saturday afternoon amid the burning winds and whirling dust that choked their throats. Because today the wind was blowing up dirt and everybody's eyes were red from alcohol and blood poisoning. They were tired of remembering. Today was payday, and a day of forgetting: a Saturday afternoon in the great, dying land of America.

And because America was dying, we were dying a little bit too. Because, for us, America carried promises of an elsewhere, promises of renewal, and we shouldn't blame her—America and her flag of snot-streaked stars—for having betrayed us. Once upon a time there was the great America and the ballads of Bruce Springsteen, the myth of what we understood without needing to know it because we'd grown up surrounded by it, and it carried us, it offered us cheap inspiration, a shared world, a dream… you still had to do it, right? America was what it did, the best it could, and you could never take that away from it. You could curse America, but you could never take that away from it, because here even two ugly men with deformed faces, trampling the clay ground in their reptile leather boots, could become beautiful and magnificent. Here, even killers could live in dignity; they could even be loved, because they were pawns in an epic; they were the legend, which is what I'm trying to describe. And I've had too much to drink, and I'm terribly sad… so forgive me this lyrical tangent. I'm coming back, back to my characters, because they are my dream. I'm coming back…

… to what might be enough, to this not-much, to the prayer Santa would mutter when she saw the reflection of those two men with their reconstructed faces in the convex curve of her crystal ball, that fraudulent sphere made of nothing but glass. The fragility of everything that could be so easily broken, because life, existence, is a tightrope. Because it is so much harder to live than to die.

It is so much harder to live than to die.

Meanwhile, Tarzan was with the lions, leading them along the path to the show. And even if he'd been there with her, Tarzan no longer had anything to protect her but his courage. His courage and his vulnerability. His love for her, like one last useless rampart.

They arrived.

They pushed the curtain aside.

They entered the dark trailer.

Santa looked up at them.

Their shoulders were huge. They took up so much space.

Who knows if what we most fear will happen in the end?

22

Luis kissed Maria. He stroked her swollen, pregnant belly. He knelt, as he often did, in front of the watermelon that had grown in the middle of his young wife's body. He lifted her dress and pressed his ear to her skin to listen to the echoes of an almost ripe fruit. Maria laughed as she ran a hand through his thick black hair and told him to be careful. With what, she wasn't sure exactly: with her belly, with himself. To watch out for danger in general. She was full: of enthusiasm, of carefree confidence. How could she not have been? Life was growing inside her.

"Be careful, Luis."

He smiled at her, picked up the backpack that contained his Nikon, his laptop, and a few clothes, then left their little house, closing the door behind him. A single-story home in a suburb of Savannah, where people could be happy if they decided to be.

Maria watched him get into their Daihatsu Charade. Life was a mystery. In any case, she would be taking the bus for her final month of pregnancy. When the car moved away, she bolted the door and sat on the living room couch. She hitched up her dress and started touching herself. Her hormones were in uproar, her body a whistling kettle. She felt this constant desire to come.

For his part, Luis was happy to leave home for a few days. He adored Maria, and he loved their life. He was thrilled by the idea of starting a family. But he felt sexually overworked and, more generally, in the grip of femininity with all the attention his wife was demanding. He needed some space. The space his work afforded him. Because he loved that almost as much as he loved Maria: his work as a journalist. And old Meredith Watson had gotten him all excited with her ravings about winning a Pulitzer.

Luis let go of the steering wheel with his right hand to make the sign of the cross, then merged onto I-95 in the direction of Fernandina Beach. An hour's drive, at least. He put on a CD of Cuban boleros to while away the time as he drove under the slowly setting sun. Life was good. At least where everything converged for the tiny part of humanity that concerns us.

23

Inside the motor home, behind the windshield splattered with dead bugs, Stella watched Father Brown take the two gym bags from the trunk of his Chrysler station wagon and drop them on the ground. He stood there for a few seconds watching as the used-car salesman drove his Chrysler into the car wash prior to slapping a price sticker on the windshield. The brake lights winked at him one last time, and Father Brown picked up his bags. He was wearing an old pair of Ray-Ban aviators. Stella wondered if he was sad at leaving his car behind.

Stella heard the sound of the RV's side door opening, then the thud of the bags hitting the floor. One seemed much heavier than the other. She could tell from the sound it made and the way the priest leaned sideways when he carried it.

Father Brown got into the passenger seat and pulled the door shut. He took seven $100 bills from his jacket pocket, folded them in two, and slid them into his wallet.

"Are you sure?" Stella asked. "It was a nice car. I really liked that model."

"A priest should not become attached to material possessions."

"What about your congregation?"

"A young seminarian is taking my place. It's all arranged. Nobody knows the reason for my absence. Once you're safe, I plan on returning to my seven sacraments."

"Your what?"

"Haven't you ever taken catechism classes?"

"No."

Father Brown offered a shy smile, then took a breath as if about to tell her something.

"Yeah?" she asked.

"You have a pure soul, Stella…"

The priest didn't dare look at her. If he had, he would have seen her blush. Modesty is one possible measure of sensitivity.

"I know, nobody has ever told you that before," Father Brown went on. "But grace touches only the purest and most corrupt of souls. There are no half measures where God is concerned. He vomits upon the lukewarm."

He was telling her this in the parking lot of an automobile dealership decorated with multicolored pennants flapping in the evening wind.

"Come on, it's time to head south."

Stella turned on the engine and released the handbrake.

"Aren't you hot in your jacket and your starched collar?"

"I'll think about that later. South, Stella. Maybe we're still allowed a little hope."

"There is one thing, though…" The young woman hesitated.

Father Brown waited, but the rest of the sentence was not forthcoming. He just had time to glimpse the shadow pass over her face. He knew that shadow well.

"What about Santa? And Tarzan?"

"Sometimes we must leave the ones we love the most."

"Your God is cruel, Father."

"I know. It's incomprehensible, but that's just the way it is."

24

First, Luis passed a group of three men by the roadside, standing on the liquefying asphalt in the sultry evening heat. With every passing mile, he spotted more and more men. He should count them, he thought, tally up the mob and write down the figure in his notebook. But he was so fascinated by what he saw that he forgot to do this. They were ugly, they were slow. They were moving toward Her, already half dead, spending whatever inertia remained to them in their attempt to reach her body, to push back their despair.

Luis Molina signaled, then pulled onto the shoulder. The Daihatsu's hood was hot; all the windows were open. He didn't have air-conditioning in his car, and his shirt was sticking to his skin as he sweated like a thawing steak.

"Where are you going?" Molina asked a man who was struggling to walk.

The lame man ignored him, continuing resolutely on his way in a pair of old, worn sneakers. Already, others were arriving.

"Hey!" Molina called out. "Where are you going?" He got out of the car and grabbed a man's arm. All he felt in his hand was skin and bones. He let go instantly, afraid of breaking what little was left of this gray-skinned creature. "Where are you going?" he asked again, more gently this time.

"To see Her…" The man stared through him, glassy-eyed, as if seeing much farther.

"That girl? The miracle chick?"

"Her, yeah… Let me go before the others overtake me. I only have weeks to live now… Please, let me go…"

Luis Molina took his camera from the bag on the back seat, adjusted the lens, and climbed onto the roof of his car. He didn't care if he dented the metal. That was when he saw them: the tracks left by all these men, a faint but very real trace of humanity. In the distance, the carnival was visible in the dusty heat haze: the big top and the rectangle of earth around it, punctuated by colored stalls. Beyond that, like the last rampart, was the ocean. And it was here, despite his precarious position and the difficult lighting, that Luis Molina took the most beautiful photograph of his life. It's often the way, though, isn't it? You need this other kind of miracle for everything to converge.

Lightness. Speed. Precision. Visibility. Multiplicity.

All this must converge to convey life in close-up.

Luis Molina managed to capture the chaos. The immensity of the chaos. And the hope too.

The hope.

25

She seemed indifferent to pain. Santa was not afraid to suffer, which made things difficult for the Bronski brothers in addition to ruining their enjoyment. From time to time they would get a tough nut like this. The solution was to take it out on their loved ones. No matter how tough they were, they always crumpled then. It was a theory that had been confirmed many times over: pain inflicted on those we love is worse than any pain we might suffer ourselves. Except that Santa was alone in her trailer: she was just an old woman with nothing but her fraying old body that could not be tortured beyond a certain point. In the hands of the Bronski brothers, her heart was like a sparrow's. Most importantly, though, they didn't know about Tarzan. Santa would have given them the name and address of everyone on the planet if they'd shown the slightest sign of hurting Tarzan. But the Bronskis' ignorance of her lover's existence was simply more proof that they weren't thinking straight. Normally, they would have waited before bursting into this trailer. In their defense, however, time was running short. It was also true that they could not have guessed such an old woman would have proved so hard to crack. Nor could they have imagined such an old woman still being so in love.

Mike and Billy exchanged a glance and realized they weren't going to get anything out of this one; Santa, on her knees, was ready to die. So, more out of weariness than necessity—as if professional pride obligated him to take this step—Billy grabbed the crystal ball and raised it above his head, ready to smash open the old Mexican woman's skull.

"Okay, this is your last chance to tell us where she is," said Mike. "It's kind of dumb, because we'll find her in the end anyway..."

Santa looked up. Blood trickled down from the gash in her forehead and into her eyes, into her mouth, trickling down her neck and invisibly staining her black dress that smelled of mothballs. She had to make an effort to articulate clearly enough to be understood.

"I don't normally like to use curse words, but in this case I want to say that you can go f—"

"Yeah, we know, old woman," Mike cut in. "We've heard every insult you could possibly imagine, believe me. One last jolt of pride and defiance, blah blah blah. It gets kind of boring after a while."

"The comments mostly make reference to our mother and to fecal matter," added Billy.

"Or our father being a monkey. That kind of thing."

"Yeah, lots of insults about us looking retarded…"

"So go ahead, old woman. What do you want to say?"

"I already said it."

Nothing, then.

The crystal ball smashed down onto her skull, which opened up like a watermelon.

Santa collapsed, delicately, soundlessly, a leaf falling slowly from a tree in autumn.

Stella's head was filled with a sudden violent pain and she lost consciousness.

Father Brown gripped the steering wheel and gasped: "Jesus Christ, Stella!"

Goodbye, Santa.

Silently, Billy placed the crystal ball back on its embroidered doily in the middle of the small table. He'd hit her so hard and so fast that the ball was spotless. The Bronski brothers looked at the body lying at their feet and walked carefully around it to avoid getting blood on their shoes. They closed their eyes and counted to ten inside their heads, before making the sign of the cross. Every life that came to an end deserved a modicum of respect. They were Polish, remember.

They left in silence. As they emerged from the trailer, the evening sun shone directly into their eyes, momentarily blinding them.

26

Father Brown laid Stella on the bed at the back of the motor home. He dampened a dish towel with a bottle of water and spread it over her forehead. They'd almost plowed straight into an eighteen-wheeler. Thankfully, nobody had been coming up behind them. The RV's wheels had veered onto the dusty shoulder before the priest had managed to wrestle it to a halt. The right headlight had hit a road sign, smashing the glass, but that was a small price to pay considering the acrobatics he'd had to perform to prevent the vehicle ending up in that ditch of brackish water as thick as used motor oil.

He put his ear to Stella's rib cage and tried to listen for her heartbeat. A pulse was beating in her neck, but her heart made no sound at all and her breath was coming out in small sighs. Was that her soul? Maybe this was how she died, like the chick in Dumas's *Lady of the Camellias*.

After gently slapping her cheeks, he gave up and lit a Marlboro. The ways of the Lord were mysterious indeed. It would take patience and self-sacrifice to ever have a chance of fathoming them.

Trucks sped past from time to time, making the motor home rock on its wheels. It was on this bed that it all happened, thought Father Brown: the miracles and all the rest. On this bed where this abandoned, destitute girl would give herself for a few dollars.

Stella the whore.

And here he was, not knowing if she was still alive or about to breathe her last, incapable of doing anything. That it should end this way, after all this trouble, with a dumb traffic accident... He was furious with himself for failing to protect her. He interlaced his fingers. The only way he could think to comfort himself was through prayer.

Before he could start, though, Stella's eyes opened wide, staring around bewildered, then she said: "My heart's on the right, Brown. That's why you couldn't hear it. My heart's on the right side of my chest and Santa's dead. I know because I saw it in a vision. She's dead."

Father Brown said nothing. He was relieved the girl was conscious again. If Stella had died too, struck down like that, the world would have lost something precious. It would have been another step down into the darkness. In her own way, Stella was a source of light.

She didn't try to sit up, and she didn't weep either. Two big tears hung suspended at the edge of her eyelids. She turned to face him.

"Father Brown? Give me your hand…"

He obeyed. A hand in yours, close your eyes, that's it. Touch it, think about it. A hand in yours, and this hand is telling you something, squeezing yours. Doesn't matter if it's soft or rough, cold or warm. What matters is that this hand is squeezing yours, asking for a little compassion.

A hand. Think about it. This is huge.

"Father Brown, I know you've been trying to avoid the subject, but listen. I don't want to be a saint, I don't want to be touched by grace. I don't want any of that. I just want to keep being what I am, that's all, and to be left in peace."

Night had fallen, and Father Brown wanted to put as many miles as he could between them and the Bronski brothers. He would have preferred to postpone this discussion—permanently, if possible. The world was vast, so vast that every shade of good and evil were able to coexist there. But however vast the world, good could not escape evil, and evil could not exist without good. Recent demographic research suggests that more than 108 billion humans have lived on earth throughout its history. Other than the 547 humans who have gone into outer space, none of them have managed to escape the planet's gravity. Our lives, our bodies, what remains of our dust and atoms, they've all been here since the beginning, along with the somewhat insane illusion that all this has some kind of meaning. Nothing escapes gravity: not feelings, not ideas. Bodies and souls are held here in its pull. Nothing gets more than a few dozen miles above us, where the atmosphere hangs like a veil around the earth, this prison from which we can see the stars. And we dream about it at night, eyes wide open, neck aching from looking up to where other realities blend into one another, those distances we will never travel, those billions and billions of miles of endless, expanding space. Father Brown might also have told Stella that our body contains almost every kind of matter we've so far found in the universe. That nothing exists outside us. That everything exists outside us. That this should be enough to reassure us. The problem, thought Father Brown, was that this girl who was the center of the world's attention was casually sweeping away the fragile certainties that had been created to last until the end, until the liberation of the soul, the soul imprisoned under the starry sky.

Because free will existed.

In which case, was God an obstacle or a superior form of emancipation?

"I don't know what to tell you, Stella. I don't have any answers."

"But I need an answer so I can carry on living."

"Grace is not a curse, Stella."

"But what about those men, the ones who want to kill me? They won't ever give up, right? Will I have to stay on the run forever?"

The priest said nothing.

"Father Brown!"

He hated these moments when he had to tell the truth, to leave people in dismay, when he had to be the bearer of the news that there was no escape, no solution other than blind faith.

"At least you can do this, Stella. You can give people a second chance, cure them, help them keep going. You can save them…"

"I never asked for that power."

"These things happen." He shrugged. "That's all there is to it."

"That's all?"

Father Brown crushed his cigarette butt in the Jack Daniel's ashtray.

"Grace is not a curse, but there's a thin line between the two."

A sentence in both senses of the word.

27

Convergence obeys its own logic: to find Stella, follow the carnival workers.

The Bronski brothers, the crippled men.

All converging on Santa Muerte's trailer.

And now, Luis Molina.

Getting there too late is the kind of thing that will fill you with regret. It's worse than not getting there at all, the irony sharpening your awareness of what you've missed.

But you still have eyes to weep.

The picture was a pietà.

Tarzan. On his knees. In his thin, wiry arms hung Santa's lifeless body: face bloodied, head thrown back, open-mouthed in stupor. The man's hands were red, as were parts of his face: cheek, forehead, lips. Every part that had touched her for one last kiss. He'd kissed her again and again, futile gestures mourning his brutal, definitive, crude, blood-soaked loss.

In the play of light and shadow, Luis Molina had everything he needed to take another era-defining picture. But he lacked the cynicism, thank God. He lacked the detachment and cynicism of the great news photographers.

He took off his faded Miami Marlins baseball cap. He grabbed a stool and sat down at a respectful distance. And he waited. He waited as he watched Tarzan in his sleeveless T-shirt, in his ancient, ripped jeans so dirty they could have stood up on their own. Luis watched the old man weep, the old man with his hollowed-out chest, the pitiful anchor tattoo on his left shoulder that, when he was young, he used to cover with a flesh-colored Band-Aid every time he performed, climbing to the summit of the big top and gazing down at the amazed audience before diving to save Jane Porter from the jaws of the supposedly starving lions.

Now, the Weeping Man was no longer alone among the carnival workers. Another man had come to lend him a helping hand.

Sitting on his stool, Luis Molina realized a major obstacle had come between him and his Pulitzer. Stella was on the run, and Santa wasn't around to tell him exactly where.

28

That evening, the twins played rock, paper, scissors, and Billy lost again.

"Fuck it, Mike. I'm shit out of luck."

"Chill, bro. In the meantime, I'm going to fill up the car and get us some cold beers."

"They'll be warm, not cold."

"Huh?"

"In this county, it's illegal to sell cold beers at gas stations or anywhere else."

"You're kidding."

"It's their way of reducing mortality on the roads."

"Fuck me, Billy, we *are* mortality."

Sighing heavily, Mike got in the Camaro and maneuvered it next to a gas pump.

Billy went to the pay phone near the drugstore. He took the coins from his pocket (the same quarters he used for vending machines) and dialed the number. It was crazy that his hands were sweating, because even other hitmen thought Billy was a tough motherfucker, but that woman gave him chills every time he heard her voice.

At the other end of the ringing phone, Brenda Moore was tossing scraps of meat to Kali, her black panther, in the section of the loft sealed off by metal bars. Shalimar gave off a strong scent of wild beast, but seeing the cat's muscles slide under its bluish-black fur more than made up for the olfactory unpleasantness. The panther was a force of nature Brenda would never tire of watching. She generally waited until the creature was fully sated before opening the cage to caress it, so the timing of this phone call—during the panther's repast—was particularly irritating. The animal's jaws tore into the raw, juicy beef, making it bleed again. Sadly, William Bronski lacked the sensitive prescience that might have moved him to call at a more convenient time.

The consequence: Brenda Moore snapped "What?" in a cold, hostile voice.

Billy felt his bladder twitch. However tough you become as an avenging angel of death, there are still childhood fears that can resurface unexpectedly, like the severe principal who once terrorized you by making you stand in front of the whole class and answer her questions.

The trick was to start talking and then worry about what came out of your mouth. Not that he had much choice in the matter.

"Good evening, Miss Moore, it's Bil... um, William Bronski."

"Good."

"Well, actually —"

"You are calling to give me good news, aren't you, William?"

"Not exactly good, but not exactly bad either."

"Then what?"

"More of an observation."

"Okay."

"The girl. Stella Thibodeaux. Um —"

"For the love of God, William, spit it out!"

"Well, she's, um... disappeared."

"..."

"Miss Moore, are you still there? What's that roaring sound?"

"My husband's in heat."

"Your...?"

"I'm kidding, William. What do you mean she's disappeared?"

"Well, we were closing in on her and then… she was gone. We couldn't have missed her by more than a half hour. She's gotta be in hiding somewhere."

"In hiding?!"

"Someone… I think someone must have let the cat out of the bag, if you know what I mean."

"You mean she was warned?"

"Right."

"But… how is that possible?"

"Well, we kind of have our own idea about that…"

"About who could have warned her?"

"Not necessarily directly. But indirectly, yeah."

"So you have a lead."

"We do, Miss Moore."

"So everything's fine?"

"Yep, everything's fine."

"I don't have anything to worry about, then?"

"Not at all. It's just that it might take a little longer, that's all. But it doesn't change anything. Not for the contract or for anything else."

"…"

"Miss Moore?"

"Listen, William, the client who ordered this job is my most important client. Do you understand?"

"I see, yeah."

"What exactly do you see?"

"That your reputation is at stake."

"Precisely, William."

"And so is ours. We're in the same boat."

"Precisely. I'm counting on you."

"Don't worry, Miss Moore. You can always count on us."

"I hope so, Billy. Because if not, the shit is going to hit the fan. And you know what happens when the shit hits the fan, Billy."

The line went dead.

And Billy wet his pants.

V

TRIVIAL PURSUIT

29

HOLY F***!

MEN SEEK MIRACLE FROM SAINTLY WHORE

By Luis Molina

It started as a whisper. Slowly the rumor spread, growing louder until it was a roar that could be heard all over the region. The tale of the miracle girl has drawn hordes of the lame and the marginalized. I recently spoke to two of the five men who claim to have been miraculously cured when they had sex with 19-year-old prostitute Stella Thibodeaux.

"I received the grace of the Virgin through the body and the devotion of that young woman," says R. "She cured me of terminal leukemia!"

D's testimony: "After touching her body, I regained the use of my paralyzed arm."

And apparently three other men, similarly considered incurable, have been given back their health by this young woman who is—at the time of writing—nowhere to be found. We invite these men to contact our newspaper so that they can tell their stories.

So what is going on here? Collective hysteria? An elaborate hoax? Personally, I would tend to believe the testimonies of the men I spoke with, because they struck me as being completely sincere.

For three days now, there has been a long march of incurably ill men converging on the carnival workers' camp on Fernandina Beach.

Stella Thibodeaux was a carnival follower and, I have been told, a close friend of fortune teller Maria Santa de Las Cruces, who was found murdered 24 hours ago.

Are these events connected? Is a satanic sect targeting Stella Thibodeaux and her friends? A series of details would seem to indicate... [*continued overleaf*]

Jeremy Carter dropped his copy of the *Savannah News* on the floor. He was lying on a massage table covered by an oil- and-water-repellent cover, his face buried in the padded headrest. With difficulty, he raised his elbow. Chaï, his masseur, immediately understood the meaning of this gesture: he wiped his oily hands and hurriedly grabbed the cell phone from the pocket of his client's cassock. Carter, glimpsing the young Thai man's firm little butt, had to blink away an extremely dirty thought that was, according to the Holy Church and our old friend Paul of Tarsus, also extremely unnatural. Since talking with Brenda Moore, his senses had been on fire. Knowing that he shouldn't be thinking about it, he had been able to think about nothing else, and this little Thai fucker, in his ultra-tight Spandex shorts, was kindling in the cardinal the kind of desires that would send a man to hell. So it was with a certain frustration-fueled animosity that he called the bitch who had gotten him all steamed up in the first place.

It was a private line, so there was no need for introductions. Carter got straight to the point: "What the hell are your little criminal friends doing?"

(Chaï lubed up his palms again and went back to work, massaging his client's lumbar region.)

"They encountered a slight setback, Jeremy, but don't worry, they're on the case," replied Brenda with an attempt at friendliness.

Jeremy. Carter didn't like it when she called him by his first name. It sounded like a confession of helplessness, a subtle signaling of submissiveness. Then again, if he could take advantage of that shift in the balance of power, maybe one day he'd manage to get her to spread her legs…

"And what about this journalist? Where did he come from?"

"Molina? Don't worry, our friends will deal with him as soon as possible. He's on the list too."

"You have twenty-four hours, Brenda. If you still haven't dealt with the problem by then, I will—regretfully—be obliged to try another agency."

"Threats, Jeremy?"

"A waste, Brenda. Untapped potential. Poetry cut down before it blooms. A task that is botched leaves us speechless with disappointment."

"You're talking in riddles, Carter."

"Believe me, I'll be far less enigmatic if you don't find that young woman pronto. I want her sainted and martyred. Fuck that holy fucker! Her fate is in your hands, and I expect her blood to be on them too by this time tomorrow."

He hung up.

Carter could feel Chaï's hands sliding over his buttocks, kneading him relentlessly, and he didn't know what to do with himself. But Jesus managed to get through a whole night with Satan in the desert, didn't he? So let's leave Cardinal Carter to his pangs of doubt and desire and relocate to Brenda's limousine, which was at that moment moving along a road somewhere on earth.

Brenda stared pensively out of the window, phone still warm in her hand. She managed an endless list of problems from the back seat of her Cadillac. It was a sort of office on wheels that allowed her to remain mobile, alert, attentive to the demands of her impatient clients, from whom she made a killing by, well, making a killing. From this car, she could give orders to her employees, who would then seal the fates of certain people considered superfluous by certain other people. But her power, as extensive as it was, did not exempt her from working for morons like Carter and his white-robed boss.

30

The moment one of the Bronski brothers pushed open the door to his bar, Malone glanced under the counter to make sure his baseball bat was within reach. In a way, he had been expecting this. With certain types—the really evil bastards—you knew things would eventually go pear-shaped. And now the time had come.

It was a peaceful morning: a young couple flirting in a booth, two drunk regulars sitting at the end of the bar, and not a biker in sight. The man had timed it perfectly, choosing the ideal hour for a quiet word. He sat on the same stool as last time, ordered a beer, and asked Malone if he remembered him.

"Of course," the bartender replied. "Nobody would forget a face like that."

"That's what most people say."

"Well, I'm no different."

Michael Bronski made a small sound with his mouth, the kind of sound you might make if there's a thread of chicken flesh stuck between your incisors. Malone didn't say a word, deliberately refraining from asking whether he was here on his own, but it made no difference, because Bronski seemed to read his thoughts.

"My brother would have loved to be here too, enjoying a cold Schlitz, but the poor guy can't catch a break. He keeps losing at rock, paper, scissors."

"Yeah, that's tough."

"Because you see… Actually, what's your name?"

"Malone. Frankie Malone."

"Because you see, Malone, Billy and I were talking about this… Billy is my brother, by the way, and I'm Mike… So we were talking about this and we figured someone must have made certain deductions and then told one of his friends we were looking for the miracle girl…"

"Sure, that's possible. We live in a world where people know each other. We're all connected, in a way."

"Exactly. In fact, the small-world theory is basically our philosophy. Our map and compass. So anyway, this friend, the friend of the someone I mentioned earlier, we reckon he must have rushed off to warn the girl that the Bronski brothers were after her… You follow me?"

"Absolutely."

"End result: we haven't found her, and that's messed up our schedule for the week."

"Well, maybe I don't know all the facts, but I agree with you in principle: life's complicated sometimes. Another beer? This one's on me."

"Thanks, Malone. And don't worry, you'll understand soon. See, Billy and I think this someone who told his friend who warned the girl… we think that someone is you."

"Whaaat?"

"You heard me. What do they call it on cop shows when a cop knows something without having all the evidence to prove it? A strong hunch? Yeah, so Billy and I have a *strong hunch* that Frankie Malone threw a wrench in our gears. What do you think of that?"

"I think maybe you're not wrong."

"Well, that's good to hear, you know? When your strong hunch turns out to be true, that means maybe you're not a fucking idiot after all. Plus, we prefer it when people don't bullshit us."

Malone waited for Mike to finish his beer—it was always important to respect the customer—before declaring: "Well, now we've solved the mystery and everybody's had his say, I think it's probably time for you to fuck off, Mike. What do you think of that?"

Michael Bronski stared into Frankie Malone's eyes, nodded his agreement, then smiled. He tried once again to dislodge the bit of chicken stuck between his teeth by drawing back his lips and making that unpleasant sucking sound, but it did no good. Taking his time, Mike rested his elbows on the counter-top, then moved his face close to Malone's. The bartender, who suddenly looked smaller than usual, reached slowly under the bar and gripped the handle of the baseball bat.

"We knew you were tough. Me and my brother, we both said that after the first time we met you. We knew there was no point busting your balls. So we decided to think outside the box instead."

"You talk too much, Mike. Now fuck off, okay? I've got work to do."

"Hang on, Malone, I just want to show you something first, then you can decide what to do, okay?"

Michael Bronski took his phone from the pocket of his Buffalo Bill-style jacket. Thanks to the wonders of technology, he didn't need to say another word: the images spoke for themselves. Mike put the phone on the counter and turned it toward Frankie, who saw a video of Margot in her underwear, gagged and bound to a chair. (Frankie Malone had never seen Margot without clothes before, and he had to admit she was in great shape for a woman in her fifties.) Billy was standing next to her, hands crossed in front of him like a choirboy, except that one of those hands was holding a chainsaw. The video lasted about ten seconds before going back to the still image from the start, superimposed with the white "play" triangle.

"I turned off the volume because I didn't want to disturb your other customers. There are some pretty unpleasant moans and shit coming from under the duct tape covering her mouth. If you zoom in, though, I think you can get a good idea of the terror in her eyes."

One of the drunks at the end of the bar let loose an enormous belch. Other than that, nothing had changed: the two young people were still hungrily making out in the booth, indifferent to the troubles of the world.

"So what do you think, Malone?"

Frankie felt an immense sadness wash over him, a sort of melancholy that had nothing to do with fear but rather with anxiety and a sense of loss. At that precise instant, he realized he'd been in love with Margot for years without ever admitting it to himself. And now he was on the verge of losing her, losing the love of his life before he'd even had a chance to tell her how he felt. Worst of all, though, Margot was going to suffer horribly. And it was all thanks to him. In this way, love had been transformed into torture, and the lover had caused untold pain for the beloved. Hence the fathomless melancholy that dulled his reactions and got all mixed up with his dread.

"Take your time, Malone. I know it's tough. I sympathize, man."

At last the bartender came to a decision. "If I give you a name, how do I know you'll let her go?"

Michael Bronski decided to work a fingernail between his teeth. Finally, triumphantly, he extracted a slender thread of meat whitened by its long stay inside his mouth. Yep, definitely chicken. He contemplated it with a satisfied look, then stuck out his tongue and decided to swallow it. Life was back on track.

"You have my word, Malone."

"That's all?"

"Make your choice and place your bets: am I a sadist who keeps his word or am I simply a sadist?"

31

Amid the great disorder of the world, with all its noise, all its odors, all its voices clamoring to say nothing important (or even amusing or worthwhile or sane), amid this endless chaos of contradictions and pointless repetitions, of parapraxes and failures and defeats, of raised hands and confident smiles, amid this touching cacophony of humanity filled with cowardice and vanity—and occasionally capable of generosity and selflessness—where we, beings of clay, are sometimes transported by a piece of music to another phase in the journey of our soul, in this pigsty of existence where we seek and we struggle, there is a necessity, sooner or later, to bring this sentence to an end, in the exact place and instant where Stella Thibodeaux is helpless to stop herself performing a miracle.

They were in the outskirts of Sopchoppy, which is not the name of a Japanese dog food brand but of a very small city (pop: 470) in Wakulla County, Florida. They'd put several hundred miles between themselves and their pursuers, but Stella and Father Brown had to eat, and Stella had to obey an even more urgent imperative: seized by compassion, she had to sneak off and fornicate in the bathroom of a Kentucky Fried Chicken, even though saving someone's life for a cut-rate price was the most inappropriate thing she could have done at that time.

So you make your choice and you place your bets: was this an act of ludicrous stupidity or of magnificent generosity?

The client was a Black man named Sandmann Johnny who had a bad case of pulmonary emphysema and was eating a $10.99 Dunk-It Bucket Combo containing three pieces of Original Recipe tenders, mashed potato poppers, fries, a medium drink, and three sauces. Stella had spotted him breathing through the plastic tubes in his nostrils with the aid of the oxygen canister in his Eastpak backpack. She'd waited for him to go to the bathroom then slipped in after him without Father Brown noticing a thing. In the priest's defense, his life of contrition, devoid of any feminine presence for so many years, had made him far less sensitive to signs of that carnal mischief which is, to other men, the very spice of life.

When Stella reemerged from the bathroom and sat down to finish her Coke, the blood vessels in her cheeks were slightly redder and more dilated, but that was all: a change barely detectable to the naked eye.

"What's with the notebook, Stella?" Father Brown asked her.

Stella shrugged. "I just like to write stuff down sometimes."

"Like a journal?"

"Not really."

"So you suddenly felt an urgent need to write some notes in your 'not really a journal' because you'll forget them if you don't?"

"Sure, if you like. But it's personal and I don't want to say anything else about it, okay?"

Father Brown let the matter drop and asked Stella to wait for him while he in turn visited the bathroom. In the corridor, he passed Sandmann Johnny, who wore the expression of a man who has been reacquainted with the delights of physical pleasure.

32

Malone found her in a derelict barn, bound to the chair with metallic-gray heavy-duty duct tape, being attacked by a swarm of flies, creatures that, as we know, have an unhealthy obsession with meat. Margot was sitting there, naked and motionless, alive but humiliated. Her clothes had been burned and were lying at her feet in a charred heap. Her body was intact—no fingers or ears amputated—but her dignity was badly bruised, her beauty grotesquely exposed by this unflattering position, her body sore and swollen from the sticky tape, her hair disheveled, traces of a struggle visible in the scratches and smears of dirt on her skin. As for her eyes, they were overflowing with tears, little streams of black mascara flowing through the fine lines carved into her face by the passage of time.

First, Frankie delicately removed the tape from Margot's face, as Father Brown did for Stella in Chapter 20: an echo that allows us to see the same recurrent intimacies, the same gestures made by men toward women, two different kinds of love converging on the same sublime banalities.

As a bartender and a considerate friend, he'd thought to bring a bottle of water with him. He immediately began helping Margot drink, in brief, patient mouthfuls. His gesture was impregnated with all the compassion of which he was capable. Margot's neck stretched forward and her Adam's apple bulged slightly under her skin, which was even thinner in that particular spot: one of those body parts most revealing of our weakness. She was still bound to the chair, but she urgently needed to drink before she fainted. The water trickled from the edges of her mouth and down to the tops of her breasts. And if there's a time avidity can be beautiful, this is surely it: there is infinite grace in the simple fact of a desperately vulnerable and fragile woman being helped to drink by a man; it is for a moment like this that I was born an Aquarius. And, in all honesty, it is for a moment like this that I became a writer.

Now it was time for Malone to free her. But first he wanted to tell her something, taking advantage, in a somewhat cowardly manner, of this woman's undivided attention. Yes, Margot was at the mercy of the words that emerged, sometimes slowly, sometimes from a great distance too, because they had been weighed against experience: all those years spent living, like a seismograph of his soul.

"I love you, Margot."

There, he'd said it. Time stood still as Margot—this woman whose past we know nothing about, whose past we don't particularly care about either, because what she is now is enough—forgot, momentarily, the tape that bound her. When someone tells you he loves you, he deserves your total attention, at least for the duration of a skipped heartbeat or a fluttered eyelash. Even if, as in this case, his love is not reciprocated.

"And I love someone else, Malone."

Frankie knew this, but he'd had to tell her anyway, because what was the point in keeping it to himself? One day, or perhaps one night, we will all die, and it would be selfish to have reached that point without declaring the truth. Because everything we leave unspoken is lost forever.

"But you saved my life, my barman-boxer. And that means I should at least consider the possibility that I owe you a little bit of my soul and my body."

Frankie Malone could have stayed there, patiently waiting to harvest the fruits of a cut-rate love. He could have taken whatever he was offered, which is often how men of a certain age see things: with less panache and more lucidity. Except that, beyond his refusal to ever retreat or throw in the towel, be it in the ring or elsewhere, Malone was convinced honesty was a virtue that brought clarity to one's existence.

"I fucked up, Margot. You don't owe me anything. I said something I shouldn't have to the wrong people, and it came back to hit me in the face. I'm not saving your life, I'm here to apologize and to make up for the mess I made."

Malone released her and the first thing he received in recompense was a slap in the face: damp palm, loud smack, blood rising to the epidermis across his whole cheek, and a high-pitched shrieking in his eardrum inaudible to the rest of the world. A violent solitude.

But then, immediately afterward: a body pressing against his, begging to be held, spasming with sobs of terror.

"Jesus fucking Christ, Malone," murmured Margot, her words muffled by the bartender's check shirt, the coarse fabric against her tongue. "Jesus fucking Christ."

He understood.

He too had experienced fear.

And that slap had been a form of love, expressed through its opposite. And fear was love. So was violence, sometimes.

So they stood like that. Margot, naked and in tears. Malone, with his cotton shirt and his devotion.

Embracing, terrified, incongruous.

Each for different reasons.

Their own reasons.

33

I'm feeling slightly depressed as I begin this chapter. Words seem simultaneously vain and like the last bulwark against disaster. I kind of want to give up on this story even as I continue writing it. Not through any lack of imagination, but through simple inertia, the comfort of art for art's sake, a novel that will, little by little, lose its plot: an eminently literary (and therefore cowardly) tactic.

But then there was Sandmann Johnny. There was jazz and carnal mischief and the spice of life. There was the necessity of music that had been stirring under the embers of frustration caused by shortness of breath...

So, that evening, the saxophonist went back to the club where he had become merely a distant memory. Which is something that happens to all of us once our old, mangled bodies prevent us doing what we do, leaving us with no choice but to tell people what it was like when we still could do those things. With no choice but to talk, because life is elsewhere. With no choice but to write, because everything we leave unspoken is lost forever.

The customers sitting at tables, the customers standing in groups, even the ones whose backs were turned, first saw him in the big mirror behind the bar as he arrived, walking alertly. This in itself was already a small seismic shock for the local community in their nicotine haze. Next they noticed that he didn't have his oxygen canister, the humiliating excrescence this poor sick man had been carrying around with him in a frayed backpack. Finally, they watched as he placed the rigid instrument case on the floor at the base of the stage where nobody was playing, because Sandmann Johnny had waited for this moment: when the concert was over, the music silenced, when the harsh light was horrifying the drunks—when the future had become nothing more than the last glass, not swallowed yet because they weren't ready to face the rest of the night alone, those final few feet of darkness that sometimes make people say life is cruel.

A stupefied silence preceded the old Black man on stage. The three steps creaked under his weight as he climbed them in the two-tone shoes he'd kept in a closet with his fading glory all these years.

Holding the saxophone in one hand, he sat on the stool where so many legends had sat before him.

He looked around, adjusted the mouthpiece, and blew into it. Saliva filled his mouth.

Tonight he felt compelled to give thanks for the sexual act that had, in itself, been a miracle, its intensity taking him closer to the stars. He felt compelled to give thanks to the boost of vitality granted him by a stranger.

Sandmann Johnny had decided to second that emotion. If you can find poetry in a KFC restroom, he thought, you can find it anywhere, anytime. Poetry is in us and all around us.

Even in Sopchoppy.

Sandmann Johnny's mouth blew, and his fingers sought then found the first note of "Stella by Starlight."

And then the notes that followed.

So let's listen to him…

That's Stella by starlight and not a dream
My heart and I agree
She's everything on this earth to me.

34

The phone buzzed on the nightstand. The little Nokia would never be a true smartphone; this was an age midway between analog and digital, and we didn't yet know if what was to come would make us freer or if life would get worse. On the other hand, one thing was certain: a hangover is and will forever be timeless.

Luis Molina put one foot on the floor, and the empty tequila bottle rolled under the bed as the journalist's cracked heel touched it. He had to fight hard not to puke.

His thumb touched the green icon.

Meredith Watson.

"A good journalist never sleeps, Molina. I tracked down your saint."

Her voice was blaring and resolute. It hurt Luis's head, and its litany of subtextual insults ("you lazy, Honduran boozehound") intensified his nausea. Luis looked at the wristwatch he'd left next to the phone. The luminescent hands told him it was 4:15 in the morning. ("And you're still lying around in bed, Molina?!")

"Sopchoppy," said Meredith, getting straight to the point. "A musician by the name of Sandmann Johnny. Tenor saxophonist who used to play Birdland in his glory days."

"How did you do it, Mrs. Watson?"

"How do you think an ugly bitch like me managed to survive in this world, Molina? Come on, move your ass!"

"It's just that I promised my wife I'd go home and —"

"Do you want this fucking Pulitzer or not, Molina? You are now my last hope of greatness. The sky's the limit for you. So drink some coffee and get to work, you South American slacker!"

She hung up, but her arthritic fingers wouldn't let go of the receiver. Jesus, it had to be a damn Honduran, didn't it? She—a pure, proudly inbred, Mormon WASP—had to end up betting everything on a sturdy, dark-skinned Honduran.

Meredith Watson lit a cigarette.

On the other end of the line, Luis Molina rushed to the bathroom to puke up his guts.

35

It would take a gifted nature writer to truly evoke the beauty of that morning on the banks of the Apalachicola River. Father Brown had breathed in the dawn scents as soon as he woke, he had listened to the fragments of sound as if they were so many invitations to the priests' paradise. Finally he'd gotten up, crawling out of the one-person tent in which he preferred to sleep and walking down to the village to buy some groceries and the local paper. Now he'd swapped his clergyman's clothes for a pair of jeans and a denim shirt, there was nothing in his appearance to suggest he was anything other than a blue-eyed killer. The gray brush cut, the slightly stooping shoulders, the deep lines etched in his face... everything about him screamed ex-military. Not that this bothered the local storekeepers, who were more reassured than disturbed by such a look. Most of them had a National Rifle Association sticker in one corner of their shop window.

Back at the motor home, parked at the edge of the forest and close to the river, James Brown (I know, I know, it still sounds funny, but you'll get used to it) made coffee, eggs, and bacon, then warmed up some pancakes before drowning them in maple syrup. He'd set up the camping stove under a giant sequoia, away from the vehicle, because he didn't want to wake Stella. He took his time, reading the newspaper as he sat on a folding chair, then smoking two cigarettes and drinking a whole pot of coffee on his own.

And now, Stella.

He folded the newspaper and went over to wake her. He'd thought a few days in the countryside would do them good, but he'd been wrong. A quick glance at pages two and three of the *Savannah News* had been enough to disabuse him of that idea, and to make his coffee taste more bitter than usual.

Father Brown quietly opened the door of the motor home—he didn't want to scare her: the poor kid had been through enough of that already—and walked over to the bed. The sheets were all twisted around her body, her firm little butt poking out at him. It was hard, sometimes, to be a man, to keep one's urges under control. But not for nothing had Father Brown been a Navy SEAL. Their motto, "The only easy day was yesterday," was a concrete application of Murphy's Law. In other words: expect the worst and you'll never be disappointed.

"Stella?"

He liked saying her name. The priest would have been too embarrassed to admit this to anybody, but we have the privilege of knowing his deepest desires and fears. He put one hand on her shoulder and, oh God, that velvety, creamy feel under his fingertips: the touch of soft skin was one of life's great pleasures.

"Stella?" he repeated.

She turned around, hair covering her eyes, entering her mouth, so much hair she didn't know what to do with it: Stella was the pure evocation of abundance. Correction: Stella *was* abundance. She was everything two thousand years of Christianity had tried to bind and constrain. The generosity of her body, the gift of herself, the life pulsing through her veins, the pure vitality, the joy of expanding constellations, multiplying cells... Sorry, I'm getting carried away again.

Father Brown saw all of this before him: that sleepy, dreamy body, hit by flickering daylight, and those amber eyes that were looking at him now, surprised this man should still be here to protect and cherish her. Have you ever seen Anton Romako's little oil painting, *Le Faune et la Nymphe?* That's what they looked like, this pair. It's true, there are some things painting does better than literature: we must stay humble. From now on, I think, we're just going to call him Brown.

"Breakfast's ready. Get dressed."

"Is it sunny out?"

"Yep."

"So it's a nice day."

"Depends who's asking."

Stella could tell he was trying to remain patient, but she detected a hardness in his tone. Or maybe something subtler and more hurtful: annoyance.

"What's wrong, James?"

Brown put the newspaper on the bed and opened it to the double-page spread that had ruined his coffee: a photograph of Sandmann Johnny with his sax, a cigarette between his lips. The caption read: *After being miraculously cured, the most famous phthisic in jazz is playing again.* The article had been written by that Honduran journalist again (according to the UN, 77 percent of Hondurans lived in poverty). The girl couldn't help smiling: it really was him, the guy from the KFC, into whose lungs she had breathed new life. Not a single *mycobacterium tuberculosis* remained to turn his blowing into wheezing.

"If you weren't a saint, Stella, I'd call you a slut."

"I didn't know he was a musician, I promise."

"You just can't help yourself, can you?"

Stella looked down, ashamed. Was nature the fruit of God's will or was it something to be combated and subdued?

"We need to change our strategy, Stella."

Head lowered, chin digging into her sternum, she asked: "Is there any coffee, Jimmy?"

"Coffee and cigarettes, yeah." Brown found himself smiling, although he couldn't have said why.

"You know, I like it when you smile like that," said Stella. "And that shirt really suits you."

His smile grew wider.

Life, huh?

36

Simon II had swapped his cassock for a cream-colored sweat suit. The logo of the Vatican's soccer team was sewn onto the chest, above his heart. Although the pope had probably kicked a ball no more than a handful of times in his life, he was an assiduous follower of the Holy See women's team. He liked to watch the girls move in their fitted yellow jerseys. Their determination, their youth, and their tensed thigh muscles under those tight white shorts gave him back his faith in humanity.

Simon II was walking on the gym's treadmill. He'd set the machine to level five (out of ten) with a ten percent incline because he wanted to work on his calves. He was sweating profusely. Without his cassock, the heelpieces of his white loafers, and the usual glorifying pomp, he looked like what he was: a chubby, bald man of average height.

Otto Mühl stood a little way from the treadmill, holding an iPad and taking note of the pope's comments and decisions. The secretary was not allowed to sit down while His Holiness was exercising. He too was wearing thick-soled running shoes. Sometimes he had to stand like that for two hours without flagging. Simon II was insistent on walking until exhaustion. More often than not, he went into a sort of ambulatory trance as he ranted about a range of issues, from the prosaic (the gastronomic fad of serving twenty-four Burgundy snails as part of the evening meal) to the ethical (incorporating the concept of artificial intelligence into the Gospel According to John). Simon II was the kind of man who worked out purely to burn the calories he planned to ingest, pigging out to such excess that he tended to regret it afterward—hence the expiatory gym sessions between the last banquet and the next. As a pious Catholic, Otto Mühl was prepared to embrace the torments of his lower back and his knees, offering his pain as an act of contrition that he prayed would help soothe the pains of all his brothers and sisters with terminal diseases, dying in understaffed hospitals.

Soon the secretary was on the verge of fainting, and he managed to stay standing only by the grace of silent prayers. St. Francis of Assisi's was one of his favorites: *Lord, make me an instrument of your peace: where there is hatred, let me sow love; where there is injury, pardon; where there is —*

"Otto?!" yelled Simon II.

Adrenaline surged through the secretary's body like a slap to the soul. His flow of goodness faltered, making him drop his stylus and necessitating a painful genuflection to recover it. Otto Mühl composed himself, smiled deferentially at His Holiness, and apologized for his momentary inattentiveness. Deep down, though, he knew the worst was probably yet to come.

Breathless, his eyes glazed with the strain and the prospect of a long hot shower followed by a 2,000-calorie dinner, the pope finally touched on the touchiest of subjects.

"So where are we with that girl in America?"

"That girl in America?"

"Are you feeling okay, Otto?"

It was true that the treadmill's hypnotic whirring sound could damage the phatic function, but, in reality, attempting to stall for time in this way always came off as slightly pathetic. Besides, what was the point? The inevitable could not be avoided. The secretary was left with no option but to run a finger round the inside of his starched Roman collar and to surrender, to reveal his true self: the face of a sixty-five-year-old man, miraculously unwrinkled but a rather odd shade of yellow from all his fretting.

"Otto!"

"There have been three new cases in the last seventy-two hours…"

Simon II hesitated. Unfortunately the rubber conveyor belt beneath his feet continued rolling at the same pace, causing the pope to stumble before catching himself, watched helplessly by his secretary, who was too slow, too far away to offer him a helping hand.

Panting, His Holiness said: "And... And what is Cardinal Carter doing? Wasn't he supposed to, um, tactfully deal with this situation?"

"I have not heard from him, Your Highn... I mean Your Holiness."

"But people are talking about it? It must be making waves by now..."

"Um."

"Tell me!"

"There is a reporter covering the story, yes."

"A reporter? You mean a shit-stirrer! Otto, my pedometer is showing 35,227 steps. Correct?"

"That's correct: His Holiness has been walking for an hour and forty-seven minutes."

"Good."

Simon II turned off his torture device and shakily climbed down. He grabbed the white towel folded on the stool. His ruddy face disappeared under thick, fluffy cotton.

"Get Carter on the phone."

"Sorry?"

The pope's round face reappeared. Otto Mühl no longer knew if he venerated or hated this apostolic countenance. Those little eyes of his, my God, those little eyes filled him with fear and trembling.

"I said: get Carter on the phone *subito*! That idiot's ruining everything: my workout *and* my dinner. Oh, there's going to be hell to pay..."

37

In extreme situations, Navy SEALS are conditioned not to look any farther into the future than the next thirty minutes. It's a basic survival tactic. Stella didn't understand why Brown, whether he was a soldier of Christ or the US military, was ordering her to leave behind anything inessential. For her, the bare essentials were equivalent to a fifty-pound backpack.

"It's still too heavy," he said, crouching and starting to throw away everything they could do without. "You can keep your toiletry bag."

"That's so kind of you."

"You're welcome."

Next, he put the bundles of banknotes in a small baggie, which he wrapped with adhesive tape. He shoved this package into an inside pocket of Stella's backpack. He did the same with his own money before buttoning up his shirt pocket. "With this, we can travel light," he said, tapping the pocket. His shoulder bag was practically empty apart from the firearms it contained. He refused to show these to Stella because he didn't want to scare her.

"Okay, great. Now what?"

"I drive while you sit quietly in the passenger seat."

"I don't understand any of this."

"Don't worry, I'll take care of everything. Okay?"

Brown drove along a series of rough dirt tracks that took them deeper into the delta of the Apalachicola River. When he came to a low bluff above some marshes, he cut the engine and told Stella to get out and take the bags. Once she was far enough away, he stepped on the gas and jumped out at the last second, rolling along the ground like someone who'd done that kind of thing before. The motor home went over the edge before plunging, thirty feet below, into the muddy foam of the water, giving the alligators a fright. Stella watched in horror as the vehicle was slowly swallowed by the quicksand. In less than ten minutes, it was gone. It reminded her of that scene from *Psycho*, except that an RV takes longer to sink and the whole thing was less glamorous than in the movie.

"You... You destroyed my home, James Brown. You. Destroyed. My. Home."

"Well, that's what you get for fornicating with a jazz musician in the KFC restroom, Stella Thibodeaux."

38

His Holiness is pissed, thought Jeremy Carter. And that's not good for my career.

The next pope was expected to come from the American continent. The northern part, if possible.

His Eminence is pissed, thought Brenda Moore. And that's not good for business.

The Vatican was threatening to find a more efficient service provider for its dirty work.

The boss is pissed, thought the Bronski brothers. And that's not good for our reputation.

Brenda had already mentioned the possibility of outsourcing the job to some Mexicans from the Jalisco cartel, whose specialties included decapitation and dismemberment.

Pyramid power or Ponzi scheme.

In mathematical terms, if one person pisses off six other people, who in turn piss off six other people (and so on), it can be observed that by the fourteenth iteration, the number of people involved is more than the population of the world.

Therefore: it's easy to piss everyone off.

QED.

What they needed to do was stop the bleeding. Which meant a certain number of people had to die. Quickly.

The six guys who'd been miraculously cured + Molina + Brown + Stella = 9.

"It's doable," said Michael, putting his beer can on the bar.

"Ten," William corrected him as he lit a cigarette. "You're forgetting the young Christ who almost broke our window and tried to scam us out of ten bucks."

"True," admitted Mike.

"And you know what?" added Billy. "You and me, we've always preferred even numbers."

"You're not wrong," agreed Mike. "Symmetry brings balance."

39

Brenda Moore was taking matters into her own hands. She was setting priorities and distributing tasks for maximum efficiency. There weren't that many different ways of doing so. As she stubbed out her cigarette in the ashtray, she observed once again that life was often banal.

Events and dramas are rare in most existences, with man spending the small change of his days and his contradictions along the way and without much fanfare. (I'm sorry for interrupting you,

Brenda, but Alice Rivaz expressed this idea so perfectly that I thought it deserved a brief literary foray.)

Anyway, back to the story...

Protocol dictates that you shut down the information and trace it back to its source.

A well-maintained and recently repainted shotgun shack. Debts more or less paid off. Two packs of cigarettes per day. Microwaved TV dinners. And a tomcat to relieve the loneliness of her evenings. This was Meredith Watson's life.

Her entire life, other than her passion for the newspaper she edited.

You have to wonder why some people insist on having children, thought Brenda as she got out of her Cadillac. She'd never understood exactly what the point of life was. Then again, she didn't want to spit on her stock-in-trade.

Sometimes she had no choice but to take care of certain cases personally. She liked to keep in touch with the practical side of the job, because she didn't want to lose her touch. If you delegated everything, it was easy to forget the reality of life on the ground: the price of a pint of milk, for example, or a subway ticket.

Brenda didn't want to lose sight of how difficult it was to take a life, to stop the proudly beating heart in the chest of an old Mennonite woman.

The simplest solution was to go through the back door, the one people in movies never bothered to lock. The kitchen was immaculate, the dish towels neatly folded, the plates washed and lined up on the drainer. Other than the persistent smell of nicotine, the little house was perfectly clean and tidy. The discreet charm of the OCD.

She walked through to the living room, unconcerned by the clicking of her heels on the floorboards. Brenda Moore went wherever and whenever she wanted; nobody could stop her once she'd decided your time was up.

But it was also possible to surprise her. And, my word, some people had a real flair for this kind of thing. It was one of the most exciting aspects of the job: discovering the different ways people faced up to their impending death, and with how much dignity. In the present case, Meredith Watson was sitting in an armchair waiting for her with a shotgun lying across the mohair blanket that covered her meager lap.

Brenda came to a halt a few feet from the old journalist, who sat like a sculpture in the dim glow from a floral lampshade. There was still life in this still life, thought Brenda. But not for long.

"You're very beautiful," said Meredith in her gravelly voice. "Women always are when they get to live the life they want."

"No regrets?"

"And no remorse. It's more difficult, though. Choosing what you want always means making others suffer."

"Put down your gun, Meredith. I'm here as a friend. Or as much of one as I can be."

"You want to offer me a deal?"

"Call your Honduran. If he stops his investigation of Stella Thibodeaux, I'll let you live for as long as your lung cancer gives you. I'm guessing five years max? What do you say?"

Meredith Watson let these words fall in silence, the invisible letters scattered across the floor, the sounds vanishing into the void that awaits us all. Five years. And what would she do with them? Probably what she'd always done, even if they were her last five years. Her eyes moistened. The last time she'd cried, she couldn't have been more than six or seven. Without letting go of her shotgun, she took a handkerchief from her bosom and wiped her eyes. Then she blew her nose and picked up the phone receiver from the table near the armchair.

Brenda watched patiently as she dialed the number. She could hear the distant ringing from the receiver in the old woman's hand.

Yes, Meredith knew she wouldn't do anything in those five years that she hadn't already done.

"Molina? Can you hear me? Good, now listen carefully: whatever happens to me, you keep going with this investigation, even if your life is threatened, you understand? Never give up, Molina!"

Meredith Watson dropped the receiver, aimed her gun, and shot Brenda Moore at point-blank range. The assassin gave a small cry of pain as she fell backward. But it was the old editor who slumped in her chair. Her head fell onto her chest, a knife blade in her carotid artery.

Brenda climbed to her feet, walked over to the body, took a cigarette from the pack on the table, and lit it. She smoked half of it, then crushed it under her heel. She pulled her double-bladed Ka-Bar knife out of the old woman's neck and gently closed her eyelids. The blood flowed slowly and silently from the wound. Brenda leaned down and kissed her forehead. Meredith's gray hair smelled of cigarettes and dry shampoo.

Brenda Moore put the receiver back in its cradle, took a handkerchief from her pocket, and wiped her prints before leaving the house through the front door. Her Cadillac was waiting for her on the street outside.

The impact of the cartridge had ruined the jacket of the Balenciaga suit she wore over her bulletproof vest. In other circumstances, this would have made her angry. But she threw the jacket away without a second thought.

She hadn't lost her touch. She was still faster with a knife than anyone with a shotgun.

40

The Bronski brothers found Robert Smith asleep in his car. They set fire to it, purifying his guilty feelings in the flames.

They came upon the young Christ hitchhiking on the shoulder of an interstate. A quick jerk of the steering wheel left him dead, with about thirty fractured bones.

They waited for Sandmann Johnny outside the Maya Club and injected him with a lethal, Charlie Parker-sized dose of heroin.

You get the idea. Let's move past the other three guys who'd been cured by Stella, since we haven't met them anyway. Although I will add that the two brothers provided each of them with a personalized exit plan, based on the variables of time, place, and social context. In other words, they did the best they could with the resources at hand.

The Bronski brothers had suffered a moment of self-doubt, and there's nothing better than action to restore your confidence. They got back to what they knew best.

That night, at the motel, Billy dutifully wrote down the name of each target in his notebook, along with the MO employed. Unbeknownst to either of them, he was doing the exact same thing as Stella. This was their way of remembering, since frequency can often lead to forgetfulness.

And since we are now on Chapter 40, one of the brothers' beloved even numbers, I propose that we take a break here and move on to Part VI of this American crime novel written by a Swiss man.

VI

ANGELS OF DEATH

41

"Maria?"

"Luis?! At last! *Amorcito*, where are you? My phone's not showing your number."

"I'm at a pay phone."

"Why? Luis, is everything okay?"

"No, you first. How are you, *querida*?"

"Getting bigger. The doctor told me it'll happen soon, two or three days. When are you coming home? Why haven't you been calling me? I'm worried, Luis."

"I'm alive. I'm talking to you, aren't I? Everything's fine, my love."

"You're lying. You're lying and I want you."

"You know how sometimes, in life or in a novel, one person will say to another person: 'Don't ask questions'?"

"Yeah. So?"

"Well, I'm saying it now."

"Is this about your investigation? Luis, forget it—you're going to be a father, for God's sake! I don't want to be a single mom."

"I'm scared, Maria."

"Luis!"

"I'm scared, but I can't turn back now. I have to find this girl. I mean, she's a saint. She's a saint and she *exists*. When will I ever get another chance to interview a saint, Maria? It's a story in a million!"

"I don't care, Luis. I want you. And your baby needs her father, *mierda!*"

"But I've got a winning lottery ticket, don't you see?"

"Luis, stop. You're going to end up making a deal with the devil…"

"Maria, listen to me: if I don't follow this investigation to the end, I'll never be able to look in a mirror again."

"Is it really that important? More important than me?"

"No, it's completely different."

"Then prove it and come home."

"Maria, this damn phone is eating all my money. I don't have much time left, so you need to stop asking questions and do what I tell you. Promise me, Maria."

"…"

"Maria!"

"Okay, Luis."

"You pack your suitcase and you disappear."

"What? Are you crazy?"

"You promised, Maria! Leave the house, lock the door, and go see your uncle in Miami. I don't think they'll find you down there, surrounded by all those Cubans. And Miguel keeps a gun in a drawer."

"Luis, I can't fly in my condition."

"Get a bus."

"But the roads are so bumpy—what if I go into labor?"

"Wear your corset, eat garlic… I don't know. Maria, I'm running out of money. I hid five hundred dollars under the floorboards in our bedroom, near the chest of drawers. Take it. I'll call you in two days. Now tell me you love me."

"Of course, Luis."

"Tell me, for God's sake! I need to hear it."

"I love you, Luis."

"I love you, Maria."

There. Do you feel sorry for them? Or do you envy them, just a little?

Luis went back to his car. He now turned on his phone only to listen to messages. The Bronski brothers were capable of finding you in Lucifer's asshole. But with Maria about to give birth, he couldn't cut her off completely. This was his dilemma now: his Pulitzer or his family. Some situations are really fucked up. The biggest newspapers in the country had called him: the *New York Times, USA Today*, the *Washington Post*... He'd turned down their offers because he wanted to stay faithful to the *Savannah News* and poor old Meredith Watson. No doubt those *cabrones* had already unleashed their best reporters on the case. Now Luis not only had to stay in hiding to avoid being killed, he had to fight tooth and nail to get the scoop that would win him his Pulitzer.

The key was to find Stella Thibodeaux. If he could complete his investigation and publish the article, he would kill two birds with one stone: save his own life *and* win the prize.

It was hard to explain all this to Maria. Hard to make her understand the motivations, however dangerous, that could drive a man onward.

The world, as it was, was not enough.

42

Coming out of the Apalachicola National Forest, they must have lost a pint of blood each; the mosquitoes, for their part, had gorged themselves on this unexpected two-course meal. No matter how much bug repellent Stella sprayed herself with, the anopheles had somehow found untainted flesh on which to feed.

"Did you enjoy our little hike?" joked Brown.

Ignoring this remark, Stella continued walking valiantly behind him. The forest was thinning out, and Brown no longer needed his machete to cut a swathe through the undergrowth. The hellish marshes were not yet a fading memory, just a path they would never take again. But trekking through this swamp-infested forest was more than a simple strategy to shake off their pursuers. As the sky once again became visible above their heads, their emergence from the woods felt like a sort of rebirth. Muddy, exhausted, and half crazed, Brown and Stella caught each other's eye and they both smiled with relief.

Brown found a small cove, sheltered from the river's currents, and dropped his bag on the sandy shore. The sun was setting. The air was still warm and muggy, but they could feel a hint of coolness on their skin as the sky slowly darkened above them. After walking for fifteen hours straight, covering almost twenty miles, they stared gratefully at the turquoise water of the river and rested their weary bodies.

Brown pulled the little tent out of its bag and began to set it up.

"We're both going to sleep in there?" Stella asked, surprised.

"Ah, so you've regained the power of speech, I see. Anyway, yeah, we're both going to sleep in here. Unless you'd rather be eaten alive by mosquitoes..."

"We should get washed first, then... Ugh, and to think I had a motor home with a bed and a shower!"

Stella took the bottle of shampoo from her toiletry bag and began by taking off her shoes.

In three shakes of a lamb's tail she was naked. The summer outfit she'd been wearing was balled up in the palm of her hand. Brown watched her footprints in the mud stretching out away from him like a long goodbye. The radiance of youth shone from her: the hollows at the base of her spine, like two dimples, the perfect proportions, the dazzling dimensions, the artistic angles, the curves and sharp lines and the silences, all the silence and emptiness trailing in her wake as she moved away, left him a speechless witness to this manifestation of beauty. The greatest misfortunes and the smallest joys cannot possibly be exported, so Brown was the only one to experience this vision, and he could have died then and there and his life would have been worth it, whatever he'd done, whatever he'd been.

All the same, he did manage to open his mouth and shout: "Watch out for alligators!"

But this was just the bravado of a man brought to his knees by sublimity, a bowed man erecting a tent to protect them from the night and its ghosts. Stella turned around, making no attempt to conceal her blonde pubic hair, and smiled. The mud from her legs was darkening the clear water. Finally she dove under, the shampoo bottle gripped in one hand. When she came up again, the water thigh-high, Brown thought about those Renaissance paintings he'd seen. He couldn't remember which artist had painted what, but one of them, one of those seventeenth-century Italians, could have created a masterpiece from this tableau.

Brown slid a tent peg into the soft earth and tied a rope to it. His hands were trembling. At the drugstore this morning, in addition to the machete, he'd also bought a bottle of bourbon. Before he crawled into this damn tent, he was going to drink enough to fall straight asleep without letting one of his big, coarse hands touch Stella Thibodeaux's miraculously soft skin.

43

They went back to Frankie Malone's bar, but it was closed. Billy tried opening the door again, then tapped the Camaro keys on the window—in vain. The Bronski brothers didn't like it when something happened to disturb their plans. "This stinks," said Billy.

Michael looked all around. It was not yet nine in the morning, but the sun was already beating down heavily. Then, in the distance, Michael spotted the puny spire of the wooden church. It wasn't the spire itself that caught his attention but the flash of sunlight on the Taco Bell sign beside it. A ray of light had traveled 92.9 million miles to be reflected in the Ray-Bans of a born killer.

"Hey, Mike, where you going?"

"If in doubt, brother, talk to God."

44

Elsewhere, at that precise moment, Luis Molina found himself in the same situation as the twins: he didn't know where the hell Stella Thibodeaux was.

And America, as everyone knows, is big. That's what we love about it: the idea that there's freedom to be found in its vast open spaces. But its very vastness requires a direction to follow, otherwise you end up chasing your tail or bouncing around like a pinball.

So he also decided to retrace his steps.

He knocked softly at the door of the trailer. It was early, but he guessed that the man inside wasn't sleeping much anymore.

Tarzan opened the door. He was wearing the same clothes as three days before: the T-shirt with the Shell logo and his cutoffs, both stained with dried blood. His beard had grown, but it was still a dirty white color, his mustache still yellowed by nicotine. The long, greasy hair looked incongruous set against that gaunt face. He'd breakfasted on cigarettes and hooch, and his breath smelled like a buzzard's after feasting on roadkill. Molina didn't recoil. There wasn't much he wouldn't put up with to win a Pulitzer. "I need you," he said.

"I can't do anything else for you," replied Tarzan. "We buried her yesterday."

"Right, but I think there's a way for you to talk to her one last time," Luis told him, sensing a glimmer of lucidity in the old man's crazed eyes.

"Don't mock me, young man. It'll bring you bad luck." His breath was mephitic. Forget that whole buzzard/roadkill metaphor: this was like the root of a rotten tooth.

"I need you to do three things for me, Tarzan. Three things Santa would have wanted you to do: brush your teeth *really* well, grab the crystal ball, and take me to the cemetery. Will you do those three things, Tarzan?"

The old man stared at him as if he'd just been born and the world was an experience, a new place to be discovered.

"Two out of three," said Tarzan. "I'm out of toothpaste."

Molina bit his tongue to stop himself cursing.

45

The young seminarian had been crucified: head bowed, chin resting on his sternum, as unconscious and motionless as the statue of Christ beside it. Michael and Billy were sitting in the front row of pews, close to the altar, eyes raised to this reincarnation of Our Savior.

Billy wiped his right eye. "It's beautiful," he said. "It looks exactly like Him."

"You've always been sensitive to the way things appear, but you shouldn't believe your eyes. That son of a bitch didn't tell us everything."

"But surely you can see that he —"

The Bronski brothers had stripped the man naked to make the whole thing more real, and... well, I'm going to be blunt here. Things got *really* real. The combination of fear and pain, when the nails and thorns the brothers had taken from the statue had been hammered into the seminarian's flesh, had caused their victim to shit himself.

"He doesn't know anything else," insisted Billy. "I'm sure of it. They deliberately didn't tell him what they were doing."

The twins stood up and went into the vestry.

"Maybe we should have started in here," suggested Billy.

"You're right. But what could we do, bro? Sometimes the red mist descends. We're only human."

They searched the vestry and found two things:

a) The cassette still in the video recorder.

"Hey, that's us!" exclaimed Billy, watching the security footage.

"Malone must have come here."

"Yup."

"Are you joining the dots, bro?"

"Malone showed this to the padre, and he warned the girl we were after her. We are both cause and consequence."

"Which means the padre knows who we are. And if he knows us, then we must know him too."

b) The photograph of said padre that came fluttering out of a ransacked drawer: Father Brown in combat gear, his face painted black and green. Even disguised like that, though, there was no doubt it was him.

"You recognize him?" asked Billy.

"James Brown."

(You're starting to get used to it, right?)

"Even back then, I guessed he was hiding something under his cassock. Like another life…"

"Well, at least we know who we're dealing with now."

"An ex-Navy SEAL… Fuck, now I understand why this job has gotten so complicated."

"But maybe we have the advantage now? Because we know that he doesn't know that we know."

"Whoa, that's kind of a mindfuck, Mike, but I'll trust you on that."

"Did you remember to fill the gas can in the trunk, bro?"

"Yeah, of course. I'm always ready for a good blaze."

"Oh, you can trust me on that score too."

46

Later that sweltering afternoon, Tarzan placed the crystal ball on Santa's grave. The mound of freshly dug earth was already starting to crack in the heat. Tarzan stood up, knees creaking. He wasn't so much sweating as oozing alcohol, like a squeezed sponge. It was hard to believe such a shriveled old man could disgorge so much liquid.

"They should have planted a few trees," said Luis, looking around at the hundreds of desolate, twisted old crosses rising from the earth.

"It's a cemetery for the poor," Tarzan replied. "A cemetery for poor Americans. I'd rather have had her cremated, but Santa was always horrified by that idea. She said that whatever was left in the urn was mostly ashes from the coffin and it was ridiculous to mourn a pile of burned wood…"

Once Tarzan got onto the subject of Santa, it was hard to shut him up.

"So what now?" the old man asked.

"We wait for her to manifest."

"What, in broad daylight? And with nothing to drink?"

"I don't have any other ideas, Tarzan. I'm chasing a chimera."

"Well, maybe you shouldn't. The chimera is an evil creature."

"And you honestly believe we live in a world of goodness?"

The old man shrugged. "I was just saying. Give me some cash, I'm going to get us something to drink… Is that all? Come on, young man, go big or go home."

Tarzan stuffed the two bills into his pocket and walked away. Luis Molina wondered where the old man was going to find something to drink amid all this desolation. But apparently Tarzan knew his geography, and he walked out of the cemetery. In his sandals, thought Molina, he looked like a poor man's Hermes.

Molina was sweating too, and he ended up taking off his shirt: he figured he might as well get sunburned. His Hermes analogy was truer than he realized. His Greco-Latin sensibility was guiding him along the narrow path of intuition, that blurred line between culture and civilization.

Both he and the Bronski brothers were in search of an oracle.

An answer, in other words.

Tarzan came back a half hour later, carrying a parasol bearing the logo of a famous beer brand and two bottles of mezcal.

"The sun umbrella's a great idea, Tarzan, but… where's the water?"

"No water," Tarzan said with a shrug, planting the parasol in Santa's burial mound. The two men sat in its welcoming shade. Tarzan unscrewed his bottle, poured some onto the ground for his subterranean lover, then drank his first mouthful. He didn't even grimace.

"Santa took me once to San Juan Chamula, in Mexico. The old women there go to a big church that's now used as a place of atonement, and they get drunk. The church is full of statues of saints among crude sculptures of animal totems. They attach fragments of mirrored glass to the statues, and they drink booze mixed with Coke while staring at the reflections of their mouths. That's their way of confessing their sins or asking for forgiveness, and they do this until they're completely wasted and they fall asleep on the floor."

"Why Coke?"

"So they can belch. That's their way of getting rid of their sin."

"We don't have any mirrors."

"We'll make do, Luis. Drink until you reach the bottom of that bottle, swallow the worm, and black out."

"That could kill us, Tarzan. You know that, right? Getting drunk and dehydrated in this heat —"

"That's up to Santa to decide. If you're ready to go all the way, you'll get your answer. That's what she always told me. Take it or leave it."

The road to the Pulitzer Prize could be dangerous and was bound to take some strange turns. Molina had already gotten used to Tarzan's foul breath, so clearly anything was possible. He unscrewed the mezcal bottle's lid, then hesitated. The mere smell of it made him want to throw up. "I'm more of a tequila guy," he said.

"Just shut up and drink."

47

So, pursuing a train of thought both rational and Christian (and no, that's not an oxymoron: see Doubting Thomas's "Except I shall see in his hands the print of the nails, I will not believe," or St. Benedict of Nursia's "Ora et Labora"—and there are others), the Bronski brothers had gone to the house of God, guided by a Cartesian faith (and perhaps also Carl Gustav Jung's theory of synchronicity for the sunlight reflecting from the Taco Bell sign, a sort of pop culture of random chance), then they had made their two discoveries in the vestry, before making the following deductions:

1) They should be on the lookout for a Beauty and the Beast-style couple behind the wheel of a motor home.

2) Except said couple had probably already changed their vehicle.
3) So they should contact Brenda Moore and ask her to mobilize her army of snitches, with priority given to gas stations and used car lots within a 100-mile radius of the site of the last miracle: Sopchoppy.

And I say unto you: it will bring forth much fruit.

As for the other pursuers, Luis Molina, being a Latin-American atheist intellectual and keen reader of Márquez and Borges, had naturally taken the magic realism route, which, in my opinion, also contains hints of Jung's synchronicity theory (a hunch I should check).

In any case, it was nighttime when Molina finally emerged from his mezcal coma. There was dust in his mouth, and his mouth was dust. Nobody had come to wake him: this cemetery of poor Americans remained as desolate as ever. The parasol had fallen on top of Tarzan. Molina rolled it away, uncovering the old man, who was staring blindly into the void. Despite his atheism, Molina made the sign of the cross as he closed Tarzan's eyes. So the attempt had failed in every way possible: Santa had not come to visit the living, and Tarzan had crossed over into the land of the dead. Magic realism—perhaps in combination with magic Freudianism—was only good for literature. ("Go home, Molina. Go home, you Honduran loser, and give up all your dreams of greatness.")

Then again, you shouldn't believe all your negative thoughts either. Sometimes the pinball machine grants you an extra ball.

As he reached down to pick up his pack of cigarettes, Luis Molina noticed some symbols traced in the earth, close to Tarzan's outstretched hand. He took a closer look and saw that the dead man's index finger was pointing at these words: *Las Vegas.*

So we might conclude that the apparently sad, lonely, definitive expression on Tarzan's face actually hid a smile. Perhaps even one last laugh at those rational, methodical types who, let's be honest, bore the pants off us.

48

Standing behind the fire truck, Frankie Malone watched his bar go up in flames in the sultry night. By the end, there wouldn't be much left: a hot black sticky paste, a steaming pile of cow dung on the asphalt and roadside gravel. Now and then, amid the racket made by the overheated sheet metal, he would hear the small explosion of a bottle of alcohol. He had to listen closely, but Frankie knew exactly where he kept his 150-proof moonshine. All the same, it was strange seeing thirty years of his life go up in smoke: it's not the kind of thing that happens every day, and for most it never happens at all. The meager consolation was the sheriff's hand on his shoulder and the fact that, this being arson, insurance should pay him a decent sum. And there was a sort of karmic logic to this too, because if his damn insurance company hadn't made him install surveillance cameras on the property, Malone would never have taken the video to show Brown and this fire would not have been started. And when he'd paid off what was left on his mortgage, he would have enough money to start again somewhere else without too many worries. The slick-haired statisticians at the insurance company may have calculated all the probabilities, but he doubted they'd ever come up with a scenario where they got stung by their own policies. But hey, that's the power of literature for you.

The sheriff removed his hand from Malone's shoulder and spat on the ground.

"Jesus fucking Christ... First a crucified seminarian, and now your bar's been burned to the ground. The world's gone plumb crazy, Frankie."

"The blood-dimmed tide is loosed, Monroe."

"Why does all this have to happen a month before I take my retirement, for fuck's sake?"

"Well, nobody gets through a whole lifetime without suffering, do they?"

The sheriff stared at Frankie, and it was hard to tell if he was shocked by this observation or if it was simply the flames reflected in his eyes. In the end, he walked away after asking Malone to drop by the police station later to make his statement.

Frankie lingered a little longer watching the last remnants of his past turned to ashes—he thought of his old boxing gloves, his trophies and his punching bag, all stored in the cellar—then went back to his Ford pickup. Margot was sitting on the bench, smoking a cigarette and playing with a strand of hair behind her ear. Her skirt was short enough to show off her knees and, yet again, he was struck by how beautiful she was.

"You okay, Frankie?"

"Surprisingly, yeah. It doesn't hurt as much as I thought it would. I just wonder where all my regulars will go to get drunk now."

"Don't worry, an alcoholic always finds somewhere new."

"What about you?"

"That's different. I mostly went there to kill time. I don't know what I'll do with my evenings now."

Frankie took a deep breath, then said: "What do you think of Florida?"

"Where old people go to die?"

"But they get plenty of sunshine before they croak. I'm sixty-four, Margot…"

"Can I think about it?"

"Sure. You've got ten minutes. I need to make a call anyway…"

Frankie went over to the pay phone. He took Comanche's business card from his pocket. And now Frankie Malone made those gestures so familiar to us from a thousand movies: he shoved some coins into the slot and dialed a number, the receiver trapped between his ear and his shoulder. Frankie knew perfectly well who'd set fire to his bar, and he intended to settle this score in his own way. And to do that, cops and lawyers were no use to him at all.

49

Blountstown to Las Vegas was a 2,054-mile drive.

The itinerary would take them through seven states: Florida, Mississippi, Louisiana, Texas, New Mexico, Arizona, and Nevada.

Thirty hours on the road, according to Google Maps. Assuming the traffic was okay.

They should probably allow forty-eight hours in reality. Stella was hungry. Stella felt sick. Stella needed to pee. Did Thérèse of Lisieux complain about being thirsty?

Would Bernadette Soubirous have insisted they stop to buy cigarettes?

They were driving a 1986 Chevrolet Caprice funeral car, which tended to overheat, so Brown was keeping a close eye on the radiator's water level. Not to mention that it guzzled gas at an alarming rate, so it wasn't easy to make the hunger-vomit-toilet breaks coincide with stops to fill the tank and buy cigarettes.

They'd found the hearse on sale at a used car lot on the outskirts of Blountstown (pop: 2,514). The worn yellow interior smelled of death and formaldehyde, so they spent a while driving with the windows down. But at least it had curtains and plenty of space to sleep, so they were able to avoid motels. Besides, who could be afraid of dying in a vehicle like that? Not a saint or a priest, that was for sure.

North of Arcadia, they were hit by a summer storm of such savage beauty it reminded Brown of Marlon Brando. The windshield wipers bailed rain from the glass and Brown slowed down so he wouldn't end up aquaplaning across one of the pond-sized puddles that riddled the asphalt. Raindrops as big as hazelnuts bounced off the Chevy's roof (incidentally, the Chevrolet symbol is a Swiss cross because Louis Chevrolet was born in La Chaux-de-Fonds, as for that matter were Blaise Cendrars and Le Corbusier), but despite the downpour's violence, the two of them felt safely cocooned inside their sarcophagus on wheels. Stella lit two Marlboros and handed one to Brown, who was fast becoming the kind of man who regales his passenger with anecdotes about names and places. He was talking for the sake of talking, though, talking to fill the silence rather than because he was playing the role of Pygmalion. Besides, it wasn't every day you passed through Arcadia, so it was an opportunity not to be missed.

"Bonnie Parker and Clyde Barrow were killed around here on May 23, 1934."

"The ones from the movie?"

"The ones from real life."

"Who played them in the movie again?"

"Faye Dunaway and Warren Beatty," replied Brown.

"Oh, he was so handsome," sighed Stella.

He knew it was ridiculous, but Brown felt a stab of jealousy when she said that. When it came down to it, maybe he'd been better off in his church. Maybe burying his head in the sand and his neck in a dog collar had been his way of avoiding finding himself in the midst of life and suffering? Perhaps it was the only way you could avoid facing reality. Hell, if by the end of your journey you'd managed to answer at least five essential questions of existence, you could count yourself luckier than most. No, three questions.

(Off the top of his head: Who am I? What do I want? Where am I going?)

"It's my fault," said Brown. "I shouldn't have shown off how cultured I am."

Stella wasn't sure if the priest was talking to her or to himself. And if in doubt, maybe it was better to say nothing. Then again, she sensed that Brown's heart had been trampled and she put her hand on his arm, which lay abandoned on the armrest. "The opposite of jealousy is compersion," she said.

"Did you read that in the dictionary?"

"No, on Wikipedia. It's a recent word."

"What about indifference?"

"Indifference is just indifference. Compersion is feeling happy about the other person's happiness."

"I'm too old for that, Stella. Anyway, I don't really know much about love. Most of the girls I knew, in my previous life, were… well, girls like you."

"Oh, if that's all that's bothering you, we can stop for a minute and do it in the back seat, James."

James smiled. Then accelerated to signal his disagreement.

"I haven't either, James."

"Haven't what?"

"I've never been in love."

"Ah."

"In the meantime, I'm happy for other people who are."

Right, fucking compersion.

They sat in silence for a while, with Stella's hand resting on Brown's hairy, muscular forearm as he drove the car and mulled over the concept without knowing what to make of it.

The storm abated, or maybe they were moving away from its eye. The rain thinned to a drizzle and the glistening road now resembled the black skin of a water snake.

Stella probed the heartache a little more deeply, pressing her cheek against Brown's shoulder. There was nothing flirtatious about this gesture, just a sort of weary tenderness.

"I have two questions, James."

"Jimmy," said Brown. "It's simpler that way. I should never have been given this name in the first place. The writer must be some sort of sick freak."

"Okay, Jimmy," Stella said, nuzzling closer to him. "Who are these two men that are searching for me? You know them, don't you?"

Brown hesitated. Would anyone really want to know the truth when it was this ugly?

"Do you want the watered-down version or the hard stuff?"

"Just tell me, Jimmy. I think I can deal with it."

Brown took his time. He cleared his throat. I've often heard people do that before articulating some horrible truth.

"I was sent to Sierra Leone on a Christian mission during the civil war there... Kind of like a Band-Aid on a gaping wound... I collaborated with various organizations there... The rebels used to amputate their victims' limbs and there weren't enough nurses to cope, so I rolled up the sleeves of my cassock and got blood up to my elbows. I spent more time carrying stretchers than praying.

"One afternoon, I was told there were still some civilians alive in a village near Sengema. I traveled there on a cart pulled by a mule, along with a doctor who had his medicine bag and his surgical instruments with him. The rebel army—the RUF, which had been inspired by Charles Taylor in Liberia—was ravaging the east and the south of the country. This was 1994, and there were guys with machetes slaughtering anything that moved...

"So we got to the village and it was just a pile of corpses. There weren't any survivors, only a few people who hadn't quite finished dying yet. I gave them the last rites, but most of them weren't even Christian so they had no idea what I was doing, and I had no idea why I was there. All the surgeon and I had to relieve their pain was my cross and the last of his morphine. In reality, we couldn't do much more than weep for them.

"That was where I saw them for the first time. The two men who are after you. A pair of twins called Michael and William Bronski, who were working as mercenaries for the rebel army. They still had their real faces back then, before all the plastic surgery they got to evade international justice. They were squatting inside a hut and... They were having fun assembling a mock human body with the limbs of adults and the torso of a child… They laughed in my face and when they saw my dog collar they asked me where God was in all this… How could I believe in bullshit like that, they said, when they were living proof the world was godless?

"Later, I learned that these Frankenstein bodies were their signature, a way of terrorizing the civilian populations. There was a price on their heads. I saw Wanted posters with their photos in all the regular army HQs…"

Stella had lit another cigarette and edged away from Brown, as if proximity to his body was bringing her too close to the horror he was describing. Her shoulder was leaning against the car door now.

"And… you're sure it's them? The Bronskis, I mean?"

"I saw them in that hut, Stella. They offered me a drink, and I'm ashamed to say I accepted some of their damn liquor. Their eyes, their voices, their aura… You can change your face, Stella, but you can't change the way you sound or the way you look at people. You understand? You can't change who you fundamentally are."

"And you recognized them on that video?"

"Exactly."

"But why them? Why were *they* hired to kill me?"

"Because they're the best in the business."

"What business?"

"The business of turning you from a saint into a martyr."

Stella tucked her bare feet under her butt, took a drag on her cigarette, and looked out at the sky, which was almost as dark as the surface of the earth. Night was falling, the moon and the stars starting to shine.

"Why are we going to Las Vegas?"

"That's three questions, Stella."

"I'll show you my breasts and I won't ask any more questions."

"No, Stella! Please…"

"So?"

"Instead of hiding, we're going to show ourselves."

"That's your answer?"

"For now, yeah."

"I'm hungry, Brown. There are two madmen on my trail, you've been telling me the worst bedtime stories ever, and I'm hungry. Does that make any sense to you at all?"

"We'll stop to eat soon, Stella. I've got a stomach too, you know."

A few minutes later, Brown parked the hearse in the dusty parking lot of a gas station and convenience store.

Stella started opening the door, then froze as she saw Brown concealing his .45 automatic under his shirt. The priest met her eye.

"Where we're headed, Stella, we're going to need all our money."

"I'd rather dig into my savings if it's okay with you."

"Are you sure?"

"Absolutely. Besides, it wouldn't exactly be discreet, would it?"

"They're going to know we've been here anyway, I reckon. But I'll be careful, I promise." Brown got out of the car and closed the door.

"So you're still taking it with you?"

"You never know, Stella."

"Bonnie and Clyde, huh?"

"More or less. But at the same time, not really."

VII

NOTHING'S OKAY ANYMORE

50

Stella pushed the sun away with her arm.

The room was circular and so was the bed. This was what Brown had chosen as their accommodation at Caesars Palace. A large mirror on the ceiling suggested open-eyed orgies. Stella was used to her cramped RV, the occasional back seat of a car, the discomfort of a KFC restroom. Brown had something in mind, and even if there was a chance he might not go through with it, she felt like she had no choice but to trust him for now. He was all she had, after all.

She found the remote under the pillow and, after several attempts, finally managed to revolve the bed so the sun was no longer in her eyes. She could have closed the electronic shutters, but she liked being woken by daylight. She pushed back the sheets and examined her naked body in the mirror above. She was beautiful, she thought, so beautiful she desired her own body, so she masturbated. Legend has it that Narcissus fell into the water because he was in love with his own reflection, but that's not what happened. In truth, he thought he was looking at someone else in the water, someone he didn't realize was actually himself, a stranger he was seeing for the first time.

Stella kept going until her thighs squeezed together, crushing her hand, and then, inside this globe-shaped room, she came. The earth was round, like her orgasm, before spreading to encompass all the planets and the entire universe, her pleasure exploding in all directions, creating cyclical time as it expanded.

When it was over, she thought about Brown. She was wondering if he'd slept okay in the hearse, in the underground parking garage, when there was a knock at the door. Stella put on a pair of panties and a T-shirt and went to answer it. She knew it would be him: all she had to do was think about him and he appeared.

Brown hesitated for a second. Her beauty was so stunning that every time he saw her, he felt as if he was seeing her for the first time. It was all in the details: the delicate position of her arm on the door, the supple curve of her thigh, the harmony of her toes like piano keys sinking into the red carpet. Her feet, he knew, were arched like a ballerina's.

"Room service," said Brown, walking past and showing her the paper bag he was holding. He took two large paper cups of coffee and a cardboard box out of the bag and placed them on a low table. Stella came over, opened the box, grabbed a donut with each hand, and began biting into first one then the other, strawberry and vanilla.

"I still don't understand how you can eat so much and stay so thin."

"I have a saint's metabolism—being holy burns a lot of calories."

"Keep a low profile, young lady. You know pride is a deadly sin, right?"

"Rough night?"

"Yeah. But my sleep isn't the problem here."

The priest took the lid off his cup, tossed it onto the table, and drank some coffee. They were both standing,

Stella optimistically in the bright morning, Brown anxiously after checking the news on one of the computers in the hotel lobby.

"The thing I feared has happened: they're all dead."

Stella licked the sticky sweetness from her fingers, drank half her cup of coffee in a single gulp, then grabbed a chocolate chip muffin.

"Who are you talking about, Jimmy?"

"The guys you saved."

"Shit," said Stella, her mouth full of muffin.

"I can see that you've hardened your heart. I don't know if that's a good thing or not. On the one hand, you won't suffer as much, but on the other, you'll lose your humanity. And believe me, I know what I'm talking about."

"Well, they were screwed anyway, right?"

"But then you offered them hope and redemption. And I doubt the Bronski brothers gave them a clean, painless death."

It was true Stella had tried to be more callous, but what was the point in transforming your nature if compassion was your lot in life?

"Will I always have to run from them? The Bronskis, I mean."

"There's one other option: you could face up to them."

"Ah."

"Aren't you going to ask me how?"

"How?"

"You're going to start performing miracles again before you get labelled a fake. That's why we're here. Miracle after miracle in broad daylight. Remember what I said? Instead of hiding, we're going to show ourselves."

"Cool, so I can get back to work!"

"Yep. We're in Las Vegas and we're going to gamble everything we have. Publicity is your best protection. Once you're famous, you'll be untouchable…"

"Metaphorically, at least."

"Right."

"Hey, I just realized something. You've never seen me perform a miracle. You've been risking your life without proof that any of this is real."

"That's not quite true. Robert Smith, God rest his soul, came to my confessional and told me what you did."

"Which one was he again?"

"The one with psoriasis and a shrew for a wife."

Stella's expression darkened. "Yeah, I remember now. Go find me another one, Jimmy. Let's get this show on the road: St. Stella and Her Holy Pussy!"

Brown crossed himself but said nothing. He could hardly blame her, could he?

51

Luis Molina was in Las Vegas too.

Not a place he'd ever thought of visiting.

But it had to be done: a whole city devoted to fun and games. In the middle of the desert, built on sand. There was nothing tangible here. Las Vegas was a mirage.

Molina had found a cheap room at the Palms Place Hotel. Well, there was practically nothing here but hotels. According to Trivago, the Palms Place had an overall rating of 8.4 out of 10 (very good). The 15,923 reviews described it as "extremely comfortable" and "extremely clean." It wasn't on the famous Strip, but he was only a mile and a half from the fountains of Caesars Palace.

The convergences were converging.

Molina tested the mattress, sniffed the pillow to check it was freshly washed, and ran a finger along the edge of the nightstand: so this was what it was like to stay in an extremely comfortable and extremely clean room. One more new experience to add to his life.

He rubbed his chin and realized his beard had grown thicker. The bags under his eyes were now like a pair of oversize suitcases. He'd driven for more than thirty hours, with occasional pauses to grab some sleep. His Daihatsu had handled the trip pretty well, but Molina himself was on his last legs.

And now he was sitting on the edge of the bed in this clean, comfortable room with no idea what to do next.

To shower or to sleep? That was the question.

And how the hell was he going to find Stella Thibodeaux among all these crowds of obese tourists with idiotic smiles and greed in their hearts?

Maria might give birth at any second, and here he was, pursuing his dream of a Pulitzer Prize—the public service gold medal with Benjamin Franklin on one side and a man working a printing press on the other. What he wanted most of all, though, was his name engraved on the medal and the recognition that went with it. So much recognition for a poor Honduran orphan in this land of plenty.

What did it mean to be a man?

What did it mean to pursue a dream?

A dream in a city of mirages.

Suddenly he felt helpless, ridiculous. This is a common feeling among idealists. Depression is their lot, uncertainty their daily bread. Awareness of the extreme fragility of this house of cards they've constructed. In the end, failure is far more likely than success.

That's what it means to be a man who pursues a dream.

Luis Molina put his hand to his heart.

His phone was buzzing inside his jacket pocket.

52

Superbloom is the name for a rare phenomenon in which an unusually high number of wildflowers bloom simultaneously in the desert. Purple, orange, yellow. It had rained a lot in recent weeks, enabling this unexpected flowering. The seeds under the sand had all germinated and bloomed at the same time. From a low bluff to the side of Route 93, fifty miles north of Vegas, you could see the superbloom stretching all the way to the horizon.

"This is all very pretty, padre, but why bring me here?"

"Have you ever seen a Siberian tiger walking through snow? Of course not, Molina. Put that same tiger in a zoo cage and you'll see nothing of the animal. The whole beauty of a being depends on the place it occupies in its environment, its freedom of movement, its deployment in its natural surroundings, its margins for maneuver. Hemingway shot himself when he realized he wouldn't be able to write anymore and that he had nothing to look forward to but more electroshock therapy. A hotel room, however luxurious it might be, isn't enough. You understand?"

Luis Molina understood after Brown put his fingers in his mouth to whistle and he saw Stella Thibodeaux appear and move toward them.

Remember the first time you truly loved someone, loved them so deeply it broke your heart. Recall that precise moment when you felt like an orphan because this new presence was now essential to your happiness.

Stella came to a halt in front of the journalist. She was wearing flip-flops and denim cutoffs, their fringes tickling the golden skin of her thighs. Her T-shirt bore the image of the American flag, so there were all those stars on her chest and thousands of flowers behind her back. And the rocky desert horizon, and the vast sky, and her blonde hair shining in the morning sun.

For a brief instant, Luis forgot Maria, their child, the Pulitzer Prize. He even forgot himself. And, to his shame, his desire for this woman announced itself in the crotch of his pants. He blushed as he took Stella's outstretched hand and let her guide him toward a shady spot under some rocks.

"It's quieter here," she said.

Brown turned away from them. He lit a cigarette and stared out at the superbloom. The effect was less magnificent than the vision of Stella had been—beauty on beauty—but his manly bearing, his massive shoulders superimposed against the sky, did grant the scene a certain grandeur.

As soon as they were standing in the shade, Stella took off her T-shirt.

"Can we start by having sex?"

Luis looked at her firm breasts with their pink areolas, the nipples hardened by desire. There's a story that Giotto could draw a perfect circle freehand. If Luis had known this story, he would have told it to describe Stella Thibodeaux's breasts.

Molina reached out and caressed her left breast with the same clumsy sense of wonder he would soon feel when touching his baby's head.

"Please get dressed, Stella."

"Are you married?"

"Yeah, that too."

"What difference does it make?"

"I can't sleep with a source. It's a question of ethics. It would undermine the integrity of my story."

Stella sighed. "Brown can't do it for moral reasons and you can't do it for professional reasons, which is basically the same thing. Having sex has gotten really complicated."

Molina fumbled inside his backpack for the small digital voice recorder and placed it between them.

"What's that?" Stella asked.

"I ask you questions and you answer them. This just makes it easier for me to write my article. So... apparently you're a saint, Stella. I think this is the first time a saint has been interviewed. It may be even more intimate than having sex, don't you think?"

"If you say so, Mr. Journalist," said Stella, putting her T-shirt back on. "Seems like a lot less fun to me, but go ahead and ask your questions."

Luis Molina pressed Record. A small gesture that began his encounter with history.

Luis asked questions.

Stella answered them.

But it's actions that matter, isn't it? Or their absence. The void. We need words, of course, but the core, the heart, the center of things is what we *do*. You can write it, but first you have to live it.

More than anything else, you have to live it.

In the meantime, the interview took place.

Stella spoke freely, although there was nothing that needed to be freed; she didn't know what she was. She had never asked for this grace. It had been given to her against her will. It was strange, now she thought about it: no Virgin had appeared before her, no Christ, just this young guy who looked a bit like him and who tried to hurt her.

Once the interview had been completed, it would be used as part of the article Molina was writing about her for the *Savannah News*. Once that article was published, it would get picked up by the biggest newspapers in the country and beyond, and Stella's story would be read by millions. After that, the deluge: television, radio, social media... everything Luis Molina would say about her would roll across the world like a tidal wave.

But Stella was unfazed. She talked about her simple life, the simple act of physical love that could sometimes heal the world's wounds. She talked about sincerity, loyalty, deliverance, even if she didn't use any of those words, which were too big, too stern, too vague. Her vocabulary was honest, plain, spontaneous. And if you had to choose one word to define her, it would be charity. But even that was expressed through her way of speaking more than through the words she employed. She admitted, a little shamefacedly, that she found it hard to read and write. She admitted with disarming honesty what she was. And what she was, fundamentally, was her body.

Then they came to the crucial point: proof.

Molina wiped the sweat from his forehead and paused the recording once they had run out of words. Stella lit a cigarette and Brown went to fetch the young paraplegic man who'd been waiting there all this time, sitting (which was all he could do) in the hearse.

Brown pushed the wheelchair over the rocky desert terrain. Now and then he had to pick it up because the wheels were sinking into the sand. The boy must have been about Stella's age, his hair long and bleached blond. He looked like a surfer, which is exactly what he used to be. He had a muscular torso, and from the waist up he looked like a young god, but his legs were thin and motionless in sweatpants. He didn't really have anything left to lose now his legs didn't work anymore. Brown had convinced him to give it a try, even though the young man had assured him that he'd not been able to get a hard-on since his accident. His name was Tom.

Luis apologized to the boy—this must be humiliating for him—but he needed to be sure; he couldn't just take his word for it.

"It's okay," said Tom. "I'm used to it, man. Doctors have been touching my legs for years, so…"

Once the journalist had verified the paraplegia, Stella ushered him away. Then she pushed the wheelchair over the rocky ground toward the tent Brown had set up between two giant cacti. Christ's crown of thorns, thought Brown. Molina saw Stella leaning down to whisper something in the boy's ear, then heard the boy laugh softly.

"Come on, Luis," said Brown. "This is between them and God now."

Brown took two bottles of beer from the icebox he'd brought in the back of the hearse. The two men drank in silence, sitting on the car's hot hood. They had time to finish several bottles, smoke multiple cigarettes, and watch the sun rise to its zenith as they sweated under their shirts. It was a long, powerful moment, a meditation on alcohol and fire, their eyelids drooping and their tongues dried out by tobacco and dust.

Then Molina and Brown saw the young man standing on one of the rocks, Stella supporting him on his stilt-like legs.

They saw him raise his arms above his head and laugh triumphantly. "I can walk!" he yelled.

The words echoed from the rocks all around.

"And I can get hard!"

Haaard... aard... ard... rd...

The echo died out, but the boy was reborn.

53

The *Savannah News* sold twenty times its usual print run and, as expected, Molina's story was taken up by all the major news outlets. The photograph of Stella Thibodeaux in her Stars and Stripes T-shirt, posing in the desert of flowers, hands on hips, smiling insolently, became iconic for a whole generation. The image was used by corporations and politicians for their own nefarious ends. Now there were recyclable Nespresso pods bearing the picture of a certain whorish saint. As for the second photograph, of Stella supporting a surfer dude with frail sticks for legs—beauty combined with strength and fragility—well, that was a godsend, so to speak, for Nike and Quiksilver. Anything can be justified by anyone once ethics have been outsourced.

And since Brown's strategy had worked, and Stella was now too famous to kill, the Holy See was forced to reevaluate its own strategy.

"That fucking cunt of a priest has annunciated our ass," observed Cardinal Carter.

Otto Mühl couldn't help smiling, while Gordini snorted with laughter, irritating their boss.

"Pull yourself together, for God's sake! And I'm talking

to you too, Carter. All I have to do is snap my fingers and you'll be celebrating Mass in some miserable, muddy village in Mato Grosso, *capisce?*"

There were no croissants or coffees this time, just a choice of still or sparkling mineral water. They weren't in some sumptuous papal interior either, merely a functional annex of pontifical offices equipped with computers, monitors, and modems: your typical modern space with an objective centered around efficiency rather than useless beauty. It's true, though, that a residue of poetry was insinuating itself through a half-open window: the sudden smell of rain falling on the dry, dusty, traffic-choked roads of the Italian capital, the needles of the stone pines shivering as they came into contact with the fat, salty, seawater-charged raindrops, which fell so heavily that Rome was draped in the sort of gray melancholy Propertius might have written verses about in one of his depressive moods.

On the table in front of them was a collection of newspapers, their headlines wondering at the reality of Stella Thibodeaux's miraculous powers.

"This is just the tip of the iceberg, *Gottverdammt!*" cursed Simon II, whose Germanic origins tended to resurface when he was angry. "What is the Christian world saying, Otto?"

"The Christian world in the strict sense of the term, or the broad sense?" the secretary asked.

"The broad sense, obviously! Mormons, Baptists, Anabaptists, Protestants... What are they saying?"

"Well, there's a range of opinions, of course, a somewhat surprising palette of —"

"Just summarize them, for God's sake!"

"Um... well, for example, there are strong condemnations of heresy from the International Seminary of St. Pius X, as well as the Greek and Russian Orthodox churches. On the other hand, the Anglicans are quite positive about the possibility of a divine manifestation. If the United States were to give the green light, Great Britain would offer unequivocal support for the proven miracles —"

"Don't count on me!" yelled Carter.

"And the Jews?" inquired Gordini.

"They categorically reject the idea that the long-awaited Messiah could be a woman. They're on our side. As for the Muslims… don't even ask."

"And the sects?" asked the dean of the College of Cardinals.

"Wildly enthusiastic. The evangelists and the Jehovah's Witnesses believe unquestioningly… The Church of Scientology has declared itself ready to welcome the girl at Gold Base if she will submit to a series of in-depth scientific tests to prove their dianetic theories… As for the Raëlians, their leader Claude Vorilhon claims Stella Thibodeaux is one of the Elohim."

"May that charlatan burn in hell!" said Simon II, making the sign of the cross.

"There's even that French writer, um…"—here, Otto Mühl consulted his notes—"… a certain Michel Houellebecq, who would like to meet Stella and —"

"Who?"

"Michel Houelle—"

"Oh, never mind, who cares!"

"As for the various lobbying groups, the LGBTQIA+ movement is naturally in favor, while the —"

"No more, please, no more!" begged Simon II.

Carter gulped down a mouthful of S.Pellegrino, then slammed his glass onto the table as if he were sitting at the bar of some Kentucky saloon. Either he wanted the others' attention or he was on the verge of a nervous breakdown. Possibly both.

"This Father Brown has managed to convince the owner of Caesars Palace to make the Colosseum theater available for the event of the century: miracles, live onstage!"

"Please don't tell me people are going to see that... that witch copulating in public!" Simon II hissed, turning an alarming puce color.

"No, nothing so vulgar. There will be ten very sick men onstage who'll tell the audience about their health issues. Then Stella will take them backstage and they'll return fully cured. According to our latest information, Father Brown has already recruited three of them."

"Do they have a particular profile?" asked Gordini, with perfect seriousness.

"Other than some kind of disease or disability? I have no idea," replied Carter.

"Well, find out," commanded His Holiness.

"And how exactly did he manage to convince the hotel's owner to go along with this?" inquired the dean of the College of Cardinals.

"One of his sons has amyotrophic lateral sclerosis," explained Otto Mühl.

The pope rubbed his thumb against the corners of his lips, which were coming up in a rash: a warning sign of an imminent bulimic episode. He had already put on five pounds in two days, despite all his sessions on the treadmill. His movements were increasingly restricted by the tightness of his cassock, and the secretary made a mental note to order him a larger size.

"Oh Lord, have You forsaken us?" wailed Simon II, staring up at the ceiling.

"Look, all that's happened is that this little wh... this *girl* has found a guardian angel, an extremely effective guardian angel," said Carter. "She's being protected by this time bomb of a priest."

"Then we need to adapt to the situation," said Gordini.

"The Bronski brothers are the best in the business!" thundered the American cardinal. "They've done their job, they've just been unlucky, and if you —"

"Let him speak," the pope interrupted.

"I know that, Carter," Gordini said calmly. "Here's what I propose: your Bronski brothers stay where they are, waiting in the shadows. You, meanwhile, go to Caesars Palace on the day in question to attend the event. At worst, we'll take the credit for Stella's success, and I'll prepare a speech to that effect. Our theologians are going through the Gospels with a fine-tooth comb, searching for anything connected with Jesus and the parable of the adulterous woman. They'll find something we can use, and if they don't, we'll make something up. But before that, Carter, someone needs to approach this girl. She must have a flaw, if you see what I mean? We need to get the measure of her —"

"A flaw or a weakness," mused the pope. "You have given me hope again, Cardinal Gordini."

"I know exactly the person for the job," said Carter.

"Whoever you choose will need to get into her room and see the girl alone. I imagine this Brown character has a whole protection system set up."

"She'll figure it out."

"As for you, Carter, you should choose that precise moment to meet with this priest. I want you to sound him out, find out if he has another ace up his sleeve."

"And the journalist?" asked Otto.

"We can make use of him later. For now, leave him in peace," added Gordini.

Simon II tore a scab from the corner of his mouth.

Otto Mühl realized the time had come. "All right, I suggest we take a break for lunch now," said the secretary. "Cardinal Gordini will go through the details of the operation this afternoon after His Holiness has had a much-needed nap."

"*Sic fiat. Quam prodicta dies,*" concluded Simon II. It was done; the meeting was adjourned.

54

"It's not in our nature," said Billy.

"What are you talking about?" asked Mike, completing a sequence without managing to turn over all the cards.

"Me staring through the window while you play solitaire. Just sitting around in this fucking room, waiting!"

"The Greek philosophers debated how to become human by adhering to our deepest nature. Nietzsche considered the contrary question: how to become yourself by reinventing yourself beyond the bounds of human nature."

"That's what I'm saying: we're men of action, Mike."

"We're reeds that think, Billy. Just empty your mind. Doing nothing is a form of action too, you know. Our time will come."

"Oh yeah? Well, you know what I think? That I can't stay still and do nothing, but at the same time I'm a prisoner in this fucking place!"

"A classic example of Heidegger's *Dasein*: among all the possibilities, we remain attached to what is tangible. In perpetual transition between the past and the future. Once you understand that, you'll have no more worries."

"Hmm. Well, in the meantime, as a creature of distance, I'm going out to buy beer and cigarettes. I'm fucking sick of this."

55

Brown wondered if he'd gotten out of his depth organizing this whole shebang. He'd even managed to secure 10 percent of the profit from ticket sales, promising Stella he'd buy her a new RV while secretly hoping he might be able to convince her to give up her profession. (He had his doubts on the latter point, however, since Stella seemed like the kind of girl who considered prostitution her vocation.)

In any case, everything was ready: he'd found his ten sick men, and he'd invited the media to the event (while ensuring Luis Molina retained exclusive backstage access). The event would take place that evening, with the doors opening at nine and the show starting thirty minutes later. The presenter—who would also interview all the guests—was Jimmy Fallon of *Saturday Night Live* fame, who was flying in from New York. Caesars Palace had also taken care of publicity for the event and persuaded several artists to perform during the intermissions, while Stella was in her dressing room performing her miracles. The Colosseum was sold out, with a crowd of four thousand people expected.

The chosen ten had been washed, fed, and nicely dressed. They were all staying together in two suites, and none of them could quite believe they were here, on the cusp of a new life, when only yesterday some of them had still been begging in the street and staying at the YMCA on Durango Drive. Communication could be difficult sometimes, with the blind talking to the deaf, but the opportunity to be touched by grace gave them a feeling of common purpose.

Other than the hotel owner's son, who had ALS, Brown had opted for telegenic profiles: deaf, blind, mute, and various forms of paralysis. The audience had to be able to *see* the miracles, and it was important to consider the theatrical aspect. The Catholic religion was built on powerful, evocative symbols, after all: the Cross, the crown of thorns, the Turin Shroud, the Madonna... Not to mention the entire iconography developed over the course of centuries.

It was stipulated in the contract that Stella did not have to cure them all: she was subject to a random margin of uncertainty, so one miracle out of ten would be enough. She had specifically asked the priest to find her the sincerest sick men he could, although obviously this was not an easy thing to assess. Brown had made them all confess. For the occasion—and since, until he was told otherwise, he had not been defrocked—Brown was wearing the more sober attire associated with his position, thanks to a colleague from the local parish who had lent him the appropriate clothing. Lastly, the event was being overseen by a bailiff and two doctors, whose role was to officially certify the participants' physical condition before and possibly after Stella's intervention.

All this had grown so huge that the representative of the thirteen American cardinals, His Eminence Jeremy Carter, had announced that he would personally attend the event. And when, at precisely six o'clock, the bellhop—after passing through the hotel security cordon Brown had demanded— knocked at his door to deliver a letter on headed notepaper bearing the insignia of the archbishop of Washington, D.C., it occurred to the priest that he was maybe in over his head.

56

Brown checked the magazine of his automatic before tucking it into the back of his pants. Then he put on his black jacket, concealing the weapon. He'd shaved and his hair had been neatly cut, his fingernails manicured. His dog collar had been starched by the hotel's laundry service. He was ready for his big night. He locked the bedroom door and made sure the three security guys were in position. He had described the Bronski brothers' appearance to them in minute detail, and I think the image would be engraved forever in the poor guys' memories. Privately, Brown hoped the security guys would never encounter the Bronskis, but there was no point scaring three 220-pound, Uzi-wielding goons by telling them that.

Getting out of the elevator, he walked calmly across the busy lobby, on the lookout for anything that might blow up among the crowd of tourists and hotel guests. All his senses were on high alert, and his reflexes—trained by years of warfare—naturally returned. Once you became a SEAL, you remained one until your death. And death was prowling close by, he could sense it. Generally, unless you were in a place where death manifests itself openly, such as a war zone, it showed no sign of its presence. Death was a bit like the great white shark in *Jaws*: it moved in silence beneath the calm surface of everyday life. It has often been there for years, unknown to the laughing swimmers in the sea. No, what he sensed was nothing to do with vision or hearing. It was pure intuition. And when, as he was leaving the hotel, he saw that woman with the sinuous figure in her sober skirt suit, when this woman smiled at him with what felt like genuine warmth and invitation, her green eyes seeming to say "I'm waiting for you, sir," Brown knew he would die soon. At that precise moment, he could still have backtracked and canceled the whole event. Or at least tried to do something to stop the machine and keep running. Or he could have abandoned Stella. But he didn't do any of this. He just turned to watch the woman walk away, that supple, swaying body he would never hold in his arms. How did that song go again? Something about a long goodbye…

Brown went out through the revolving door and stopped for an instant at the top of the steps, seeing the crush of people outside the Colosseum, barely held in check by the line of police. Not only were there four thousand people in the auditorium itself, there were thousands more rubberneckers pressed outside the entrance, including a hundred or so lame and sick people who had emerged from their doorways and their hostels driven by curiosity, by the slenderest of hopes.

Smiling, he lit his cigarette with a plastic lighter. The limousine was waiting for him at the foot of the steps. The hotel valet rushed to open the door for him and Brown disappeared inside the Cadillac.

As he settled into the back seat, he thought that he didn't mind the idea of dying, so long as it happened in the flow of life and not in some hospital bed.

57

Brenda Moore walked through the hotel lobby. She'd found Father Brown quite attractive in his classy, dark suit. In a better world, they'd have gotten along fine. He was the kind of man she might easily have hired: a loyal man, a man she could count on. And she wouldn't have had to force herself to look at him, unlike those repulsive Bronski brothers.

As she pressed the elevator button for the top floor, Brenda thought about falcons. Legend had it that you should never look one in the eye in case you scared it to death. A human's gaze, apparently, had the power to explode the bird's little heart with terror.

And Stella Thibodeaux was, in her own way, a sort of wild animal. Not a falcon, maybe, although you never know how much instinct anybody has until the moment of truth.

Brenda emerged from the elevator and headed for the upstairs housekeepers' room. She knocked at the door, waited, then took out her skeleton key. As planned, there was a freshly pressed uniform on a hanger behind the door. She quickly got changed, checked her appearance in the mirror, and came out behind a cart which she pushed silently along the corridor that led to Stella's room.

The three security goons ogled her ass, verified her ID, and searched the pile of towels on the cart: no weapons or blunt instruments. The one of the three who seemed the friendliest, despite the scar on his cheek, apologized before performing a body search. Brenda let him do it, without reacting at all. "It's kind of late," he said. "Your colleagues have already cleaned the other rooms on this floor."

"The guest asked not to be disturbed."

"Yeah, I don't know if she's a saint or a whore, the priest's little girl, but fuck me, she naps a lot!"

The other two burst out laughing. Brenda felt sharp little teeth biting into her heart. Of course she was here to do the dirty work, but she couldn't help feeling a sort of solidarity with Stella and hoping that one way or another the girl would scrape through.

She gave two quick knocks at the door, placed the magnetic card against the reader, and entered Stella Thibodeaux's suite. She waited in silence, but the girl didn't appear. She could hear music coming from a radio in the bathroom. Brenda rapidly opened one of the bottles of detergent and took a syringe of opaque liquid from it. She removed her shoes and soundlessly walked across the enormous room.

Through the half-open door, she saw Stella in the Jacuzzi, surrounded by bubbles. Only her head and arms were above the water, and Brenda gazed at the girl's fleshy, sensual lips, her closed eyelids. She was breathing slowly, like someone who'd dozed off.

Brenda pushed open the door. She walked over and gently lifted the girl's arm. Turning Stella's hand palm up, she examined her lifeline. Although she had eliminated hundreds of targets before this, Brenda felt curious and intimidated. Holding the syringe in her mouth, she hesitated for the first time. This would be her secret, this helplessness, this revelation of her Achilles heel. Something was holding her back, preventing her from completing the job. She took the girl's pulse: slow and steady. She realized Stella was in a state of stasis, that she must be gathering her strength so she could redistribute it to the sick men later that night. Brenda had not been ordered to make Stella Thibodeaux's right-sided heart stop beating, but to do something even more repellent:

to take her dignity. She felt slightly ashamed, but life and death were like an endless game of chess and she was not on the side of the innocent. And sometimes, between life and death lay deception and betrayal.

As the long needle penetrated her skin, Stella moaned. Brenda pressed the plunger and the liquid flowed into her vein. Stella mumbled a few words and tried to free herself, but already her inert body was slipping back into the warm, bubbling water.

Brenda rested the girl's neck over the edge of the tub so she was in no danger of drowning. In about ten minutes she would wake with no memory of anything that had happened. Brenda rolled up the sleeve of her uniform, slid her arm into the water, and found Stella's pussy, the lips soft and fluid. Brenda's fingers were cold, despite the warmth of the water. They penetrated her, these fingers that had killed, broken, tortured, these fingers that had caused so much suffering.

What do you get when cruelty meets innocence?

Before leaving, Brenda pressed her mouth against Stella's.

Farewell, my lovely.

This girl seemed to her like an illegitimate sister, or a lover, a mistress bathing nude on the other side of the river.

A river that could not be crossed.

The Judas kiss.

58

The conversation in the back seat of the limousine, between Brown and Cardinal Carter, had been disappointingly banal. The kind of exchange that leaves both sides as losers because it has been so utterly lacking in intelligence. Or when each side has no choice but to become more deeply entrenched in their positions. The chauffeur drove randomly through the streets of Vegas, so fluidly Brown felt nauseated. First, His Eminence explained that he was meeting Brown incognito. Next he began a series of circumlocutions, the conclusion of which was that the little priest from the back of beyond had committed the most stupid act of the century by taking a position on this issue without first consulting the Catholic hierarchy. Now the damage was done, the papacy had to protect itself as best it could by adopting an improvised tactic.

"Although this wh… this girl has to actually perform the miracles first," the cardinal added sarcastically.

"You know as well as I do that she's capable of it, otherwise you wouldn't have gotten rid of the other witnesses."

"Lies and speculation."

"You sound like the gangster you are, Carter."

"And you sound like the common foot soldier of a God that isn't ours. Do you even realize what you've set in motion? The politically delicate and unstable position in which you've put our Holy Church? Who do you think you are? Some dumb knight on a white charger?"

"Don't attack Stella. I'm the one who made the mistake of passing on what Robert Smith, God rest his soul, told me in confession. I was under the impression that grace was blind, that a prostitute from deepest Georgia has as much chance of being granted the Lord's mercy as some French aristocrat. But it would overturn all your dogma—your Paul of Tarsus, your St. Augustine, your saints who are always virgins and martyrs. Your enemy isn't me, it's freedom. It's deliverance, through love, from all your hypocrisy and your propriety, your sins and your rules, the kind of religion that begat psychoanalysis and satanic possession... I've seen her do it, Carter. I've seen her make a lame man walk again, give him back his dignity. And she will be victorious."

"I hope so, for your sake. Because if she isn't, you'll be subject to anathema."

"Spare me your bullshit, Carter. Nobody uses terms like that anymore."

"Well, then, just know that His Holiness's wrath will match the severity of your sin. This conversation is over, Brown. Driver, stop here!"

"Wait, there's one last thing. Tell the Pope to go fuck himself. Or, better still, to get his secretary to do it for him. If he hasn't already. *Auf Wiedersehen.*"

Like I said, a disappointingly banal conversation, with each side entrenched in its position.

As he walked across the hotel lobby, Brown thought ruefully that it could hardly have been otherwise. And yet in the back of his mind he couldn't shake the feeling that he had been manipulated, lured to a pointless meeting to get him away from Stella.

He upped his pace, hammered the elevator button, and practically ran the last part of the way through the corridor to Stella's room. But he felt a measure of relief when he saw the three bodyguards standing where he'd left them, particularly when they told him there had been no suspicious activity and no visitors to the room except for the chambermaid.

Stella was still in her bubble bath when he opened the door. And the clock on the wall told him that, a few hours from now, those bastards would not be able to harm her anymore, that he would have accomplished his mission.

59

Sitting in her private dressing room, Stella was alone. She had refused the Colosseum's offer of its hairdresser and makeup artist, not to mention all the other perks of performing here, such as champagne, flowers, and petits fours. On the stage, young women in frilly skirts and garters were dancing a high-kicking quadrille to the music of Offenbach. This mash-up of Wild West saloon and Parisian whorehouse was a homage to the historical connections between France and the United States: the red-white-and-blue of their flags, de Tocqueville's tribute to democracy, and Auguste Bartholdi's famous statue, *Liberty Enlightening the World.* It was kitsch and clumsy, but what else do you expect from Vegas? The audience responded enthusiastically, and in the dressing room where Stella sat, feeling trapped, the sound of applause filtered through the walls as a muffled roar.

She looked at herself in the bulb-lined mirror. She wasn't wearing makeup and was dressed in her usual outfit: the American flag T-shirt, her denim cutoffs, her flip-flops. Her clothes were all clean, though, and they smelled of laundry detergent, which gave her a strange feeling, because this was not her natural odor. In the room next door, the Colosseum staff had installed a king-size bed and lots of candles and fluffy towels. The en suite shower, for artists only, had been cleaned to a shine with bleach. Stella had seen this bedroom and she thought it looked sad. It wasn't any uglier than her old motor home or any of the uncomfortable beds in which she'd dispensed her miraculous love. It was just sadder, because it had been designed with a specific goal in mind, and it needed to produce results.

Two brief knocks at the door. Stella got up to open it and Brown came in, while the two bodyguards remained outside. Stella sat down in front of the mirror again, drank some water, and lit a cigarette.

"It's crazy out there," said Brown. "The audience is scream-ing, and it's only just getting started. And the cops are on high alert because there's a crowd of homeless people and all kinds of poor working folk massed outside."

"But… what do they want, Jimmy?"

"Hope, Stella."

The priest lit a cigarette too. He was trying to hide his nerv-ousness, and it took all his ex-military self-discipline to succeed.

"How do you feel, my lovely?"

It was the first time he'd ever spoken to her like this, and she found it hard to get used to. Everything was happening too quickly.

"I don't know, I… I always used to do it without thinking. It was simply part of life, you know?"

"Everything will be okay, you'll see. Just be yourself."

There was a knock at the door, and Brown opened it. The showrunner, Jimmy Fallon's assistant, announced: "Five minutes."

"We'll be ready," Brown reassured her, before closing the door again.

Stella stubbed out her cigarette in the ashtray with the Caesars Palace logo. She pulled a few faces in the mirror.

"I had a dream earlier, when I was in the bubble bath. This woman came in. She was very beautiful, with green eyes. Her hand touched me and… her fingers were so cold. It was sweet and scary at the same time."

"The Holy Virgin?" suggested Brown.

"I don't know, Jimmy. Would the Virgin pleasure you?"

"What do you mean?"

"I came in my sleep. The kind of orgasm I used to have when I was young, when I first discovered all this pleasure inside me, this pleasure I could experience whenever I wanted, and it was like the rest of the world didn't exist anymore because all I cared about was that pleasure."

Brown scratched his head. Many things in this world were beyond his understanding.

"I don't know what that means, Stella, but after tonight you'll be free to do whatever you want. You can keep running or you can stay, but either way you'll be free, because you'll still be alive."

Stella held his hand. She did it cautiously and very gently. It was a gesture of gratitude and consolation. Her eyes told him not to worry. Whatever happens, they said, you should never worry. Because worrying was pointless.

Another knock at the door. "One minute!" called the voice.

60

The decibels rose as Jimmy Fallon warmed up the room. He had the technique of a preacher, thought Brown, who was more the strong and silent type. But America is the land of hucksters and televangelists. Here, the Dream looms so large in the national imagination that when someone tells you with great confidence that he can sell it to you, then you'll do all you can to buy it. Whatever the price.

The audience had reached fever pitch even before Stella Thibodeaux walked out onstage, wild and willowy, brave and amused. If you've heard about the silence that used to descend at Maxim's when Gary Cooper appeared in the room, dressed in a white tux… well, this was the same only more sudden and magical, more prodigious and literary. And, obviously, larger than life. The audience's yells shrank to a whisper, then an intake of breath, then absolute silence. Even Jimmy Fallon, used to chatting with the world's biggest stars, was left speechless. The doctors froze and the sick men lowered their eyes with fear and trembling. Stella was a beauty. Stella was a divinity. Stella was a goddess. The whole audience understood this, deep within themselves, in their hearts and in their blood. Brown stood to one side, measuring the enormity of the impact. His gaze landed on the first row, where Cardinal Carter sat, and his beatific expression made Brown believe maybe, at that precise instant, even he wanted it all to be true. That he wanted grace to be made flesh, that he wanted this to be something people would talk about for centuries. Forever and ever.

Amen.

Of course, the silence could not go on indefinitely. And it didn't. The applause that followed the acclamation was deafening.

Stella was introduced, and she spoke to the audience.

"Good evening. I just want to say that I love you, I love you all…"

A sort of collective hysteria spread through the auditorium. Every single person knew she was looking at *them*, one after another, man or woman, old or young, beautiful or ugly, you or someone else, and the humanity in all of you.

Your flesh, your blood.

You. Them. Me.

And this love was real.

And the first of the afflicted, a blind man, was led out onstage. And he held onto Stella's arm and walked away with her.

And nobody thought for an instant that there was anything dirty about this.

No one thought that one body touching another could possibly be a sin.

61

The crowd.

Each and every individual within it was unique.

This was Stella's gift: she made people feel unique, isolating them from the group to mark them out as separate entities, atoms.

But the crowd grew wild and molecular again. The crowd became impatient. You had to give it what it was expecting, but the miracle hadn't occurred: Stella had walked offstage with the blind man, the deaf man, the mute, the deaf mute, the paraplegic. Five of the ten…

… and still nothing.

In the wings, Luis Molina interviewed each of them as they emerged from the bedroom. He did it tactfully, avoiding the carnal aspect and talking about energy, flux, sincerity, purity, surprise. There was an interpreter to translate his words into sign language when necessary, and he'd written down his questions, handing out pens and notebooks for those who preferred to communicate this way. In truth, though, most of them didn't know what to write, what to say, how to respond.

It was all very difficult. They could still feel the warmth of her skin, the tenderness and love of Stella Thibodeaux in their flesh. And the bliss. Yes, that too.

But none of them were given back their sight or hearing or the ability to speak or the use of their legs.

The only thing that mattered to the crowd was revelation. Proof.

Only then would they bow down to her.

If not, there could be no worship, no love.

Only hate.

Onstage, Jimmy Fallon was doing his best to keep the energy high. He was using all his talents as an orator, welcoming the sick men, making the crowd laugh (albeit more and more nervously), introducing the other entertainers: the tightrope walkers, the magicians, the contortionists. He was sweating profusely, wiping his forehead and neck with a large cotton handkerchief, his bubbly personality masking the dwindling enthusiasm, his own doubts. Slowly the spectators' euphoria and expectation turned to irritability, and their impatience manifested itself in a sort of communal lamentation every time a miracle failed to occur. He reassured them by repeating that they needed to be patient, to wait, that the chemistry took time to happen. Just wait.

When the jugglers came on, Brown went backstage to check on Stella. He found her sitting on the edge of the bed, head hanging. Despite the air-conditioning and the scented candles, the room smelled of rancid sweat, an acrid odor that, in these circumstances, seemed ugly. And the circumstances, let's be honest, were not promising. The circumstances were humiliating. Brown forced himself not to think about the potential for disaster.

"I can't do it anymore, Jimmy."

He sat beside her on the crumpled sheets. She scratched nervously at an itchy red spot on her arm, making it bleed.

"Did you get bitten by a mosquito?" Brown asked. Stella didn't reply. He tried to console her by placing his hand on her shoulder.

"Please don't. Don't touch me."

Brown pressed his hands together, but it wasn't a prayer, merely a nervous gesture. An attempt to calm the twisting of dread in his guts.

"Don't worry, Stella. There are still five others. And all it takes is one, you know."

"It's like I've lost something... Like when there's something missing from a room but you can't work out what it is."

"Do you want to eat something?"

"No, I'm fine. I just can't work out what's missing from the room."

"Close your eyes. Search for what's missing."

Stella's eyelids were heavy. She tried to remember the inside of her motor home, her life before. She tried to find Santa, but she couldn't, and she felt a great emptiness in the pit of her stomach.

"Please go get the next one, Jimmy."

62

As a former Navy SEAL lieutenant, James Brown had seen this before. The ravaged battlefield; his men in pieces, begging to be put out of their misery; the carnage of a military operation gone terribly wrong, starting with the radio operator standing on a mine and ending with a retreat where every step back feels like a step forward. If Brown had to pinpoint when it all started to go downhill, he could do so without hesitation: it was when he'd left the hotel a few hours earlier. It was a vague sensation, but the worm was now in the fruit.

As soon as the hotel owner's son had left Stella's room without showing any improvement in his condition, Brown knew the game was up. They'd saved the kid until last in the hope of a grand finale. And he'd done his part, which was no mean feat in itself, given that the boy was gay. In this case, though, it wasn't Stella's saintliness that had helped but her long experience as a prostitute.

Brown had slipped away as the first cushions were being torn off the seats in the auditorium and thrown angrily at the stage. A security cordon quickly formed to prevent a stage invasion, but it would only hold out for a few minutes before the hordes broke through and ran amok in the theater's wings. Other objects landed onstage—lighters, coins—and a phone hit Jimmy Fallon in the face, forcing him to retreat. People hurled abuse, yelled insults, spat, and wept, sometimes all at once. One of the auditorium's employees, an electrician by trade, ordered the spotlights to be shone in the eyes of the audience. This shrewd move gave him and his colleagues a few extra minutes to escape. The overriding emotion was hatred. And of all the people the mob wanted to lynch, Stella was at the top of the list.

They'd been expecting her to give them hope, and they felt betrayed.

But Brown, anticipating this outpouring of anger, had rushed straight to her dressing room. He found her looking dejected at her inability to perform a single miracle.

"Stella, the woman in your dream... what did she look like?"

"Jimmy, what does that matter now?"

"Just tell me!"

"She had glossy, wavy hair like a movie star. And a beautiful face, with very pale skin."

"And in your dream, she was in your hotel room?"

"Yeah. Standing over my bathtub."

"Did she say anything?"

"She... She said if I just relaxed, I'd be set free, I'd be an ordinary girl again... And she asked me if that was what I wanted. And she gave me that pleasure, you know?"

"And what did you say, Stella? Stella?!"

"I... I said yes."

Brown recalled the woman he'd met in the hotel lobby, the look on her face. He felt it again, the chill that had run down his spine, the invitation to die that she was offering him, to die by obeying his nature: combat.

Luis Molina burst into the dressing room. His face was covered in bruises and scratches, his shirt ripped, his Nikon stolen.

"They're coming! And they're fucking crazy!"

Brown knocked over the screen in the dressing room and rushed to grab his gym bag, heavy with the burden of metal and destruction.

63

Ending is more difficult than beginning. Especially when you're surrounded by noise, chaos, and the risk of death. And it was up to him, Brown, to end it.

The three of them ran along the corridor, led by the priest. They kept bumping into walls and crowds of lighting technicians and wardrobe supervisors, an endless array of assistants, and all the other Colosseum employees. Nobody was paying them any attention now, but at this rate they would be torn to pieces in less than five minutes. Brown took the Mossberg out of his bag, pumped the breech, and fired at the ceiling. The cartridge blew a crater in the plasterboard that filled the corridor with dust. More importantly, though, everyone else threw themselves to the floor in terror.

Brown opened one fire door then another, leading Stella and Molina down some emergency stairs that led to the underground parking garage. As they fled, a series of sounds concentrated around them: gasps and pants, muttered curses, and the squeak of rubber soles on metal—except for Stella, who had taken off her flip-flops and was running barefoot.

Believing they were out of immediate danger, Brown stopped on one of the staircase landings. Stella bounced off the priest's massive back. Molina laughed idiotically, out of fear and fatigue.

"Okay," said Brown. "The garage exit is on the opposite side to the venue's main entrance, so we should be able to escape without too many problems. Luis, what floor did you park on?"

"The third."

"The hearse is on the second. I'll wait for you both there."

"What do you mean?" asked Stella. "I'm coming with you."

"No, I want you to stay with Luis. Lie on the back seat and don't move."

"But it's a two-door Charade," said Molina.

"Stella's a contortionist, she'll figure something out. Do you have a blanket or something in the trunk?"

"I think so, yeah."

"Cover her with it."

Brown took the automatic pistol from his bag, loaded it, and handed it to the journalist. "You know how to use this?"

Hesitantly, awkwardly, Molina took the gun from the priest. "Um…"

"Give me that," said Stella. "I know how to use it."

"Good. So come down to the second floor and then follow me. If anyone comes after us, the idea is that they'll think Stella's with me in the hearse, okay?"

"Shouldn't we stick together?" suggested the Honduran.

"Just do what I say, Molina. If we get split up, no matter what happens, take Stella to Arcadia, to the Days Inn. Got it?"

"…"

"I said have you got it? Repeat what I said."

"I should take her to the Days Inn in Arcadia," said Molina. "And now —"

Brown didn't have time to finish his sentence because the phone buzzed in Luis's pants pocket. The journalist didn't want to answer it, but Brown ordered him to: "You should never neglect a potential source of information."

"Hello?" said Luis.

He listened, frowning, gradually turned pale, said yes a few times, then hung up.

"My wife's about to give birth and I'm in an underground parking garage in Las Vegas with a defrocked priest and a failed saint."

"And you won't win that Pulitzer either," added Stella.

64

In reality, we're always running toward our destiny, no matter what we do. And in the reality of reality, it was the Bronski brothers who had it right: man truly is a creature of distance, suspended between possibilities and elsewheres, forever incomplete in the choice he makes in the present reality, which is, let's admit it, often pretty disappointing. That last part is me, though, not Heidegger.

And talk of the devil… There's a bottle-green Camaro, its hood painted with two white stripes, parked right next to Brown's hearse. Two Chevrolets, but models from opposite ends of the automaker's range, connected by a leap of logic: drive recklessly in the former and there's a good chance your body will end up in the latter.

And just as no bounty hunter in the old Wild West was complete without his horse, nowadays no hit man is complete without his car.

One of the Bronskis—it was impossible at this distance to tell whether it was Billy or Mike—was leaning against the Camaro, smoking a cigarette. He had long ceased to be the kind of man who cared about smoke detectors, so he'd simply smashed the sprinkler.

Brown aimed his Mossberg at the ugly assassin and fired without hesitating. The gunshot echoed in the parking garage, so loud it seemed to make the concrete shudder. The Camaro's windshield shattered, sadly, while the second brother crept up like a shadow behind Brown and pressed the barrel of a huge pistol, probably a .357 Magnum, into the back of the priest's head.

"It's a shame to shoot without shooting the breeze

first," said Mike. (Which means the other guy was Billy, of course.)

"You should do the same and just get it over with," replied Brown.

"I happen to agree, but I'm obliged to ask you a simple question first. Don't worry, you can go to priest paradise as soon as you've answered it. Okay? So, drop your gun… Theeeeere you go, perfect. You've been a real pain in the ass, James Brown. And you know what? We're more into country music than funk or soul or any of that Negro crap." Then, to his brother, he called out: "Okay, Billy, you can get up now!"

Billy climbed to his feet, dusted down his fringed jacket, and shot a weary look at the damage to his car. This was his big mistake: focusing on the Camaro, turning his back on his brother instead of keeping an eye on him. The problem was that we were approaching the end of the match: everybody was tired, and even consummate pros like Djokovic or Nadal can sometimes serve a double fault in the fifth set.

"I can't believe you walked into our trap," said Mike. "You're pretty dumb for a SEAL."

"Oh really? That's rich coming from you two, Tweedledumb and Tweedledumber."

Brown smiled. Stella Thibodeaux, barefoot and feline, had just appeared behind Mike and pressed the pistol barrel into his back. God bless that saintly whore.

"I think you've got the answer to your question now, dickhead," Brown added, taking the revolver from Mike's hand.

Luis turned up then, behind the wheel of his Daihatsu Charade. That poor little minicar had seen too much in the past week, and its ordeal wasn't over yet. It deserved its own reserved parking space in automobile heaven.

The car's tires squealed as it drew up alongside them. Molina leaned across and opened the door, contorted himself to lower the passenger seat, and got tangled in his seat belt. The Charade really wasn't designed for urgent situations of this type. But when you start writing a story, you don't always know what will happen later; I was thinking more of the happy ending, with Maria Molina attaching the BABY ON BOARD sticker to the back window of this same little car.

Brown pointed his gun at Michael Bronski's forehead. He'd been wanting to send this son of a bitch to hell for a long time, since their first meeting in Africa, but Stella physically pulled him away from this idea and shot at the Camaro's wheel.

"Let's go, Jimmy! No vengeance, no grudges."

She ran to the Charade, while Brown stood indecisively for a second before following this girl, who was full of surprises and whose shapely legs were disappearing into the cramped back seat. The Daihatsu began moving forward and Brown readied himself to jump into it.

Bang.

What ultimately propelled him inside the car was a bullet in his lower back. The car door slammed into a concrete pillar and banged shut behind him.

Billy the sharpshooter had drawn and hit his target, and he was still aiming the gun in that direction as the Charade vanished from his field of vision.

"That's what you get for being too Christian, Stella," said Brown with a laugh.

But it was a laugh of pain and despair.

65

Their flight was all very Cowboys and Indians, except that the Washoe, the Paiute, and the Shoshone tribes are merely a shadow of what they were back in the glory days when this land still had no name.

As they emerged from the parking garage, Molina took a right, with a CinemaScope vision of the pursuing mob in his rearview mirror. Stella turned to look through the back window and saw police vans with water cannons mounted on top to disperse the rioters. After that, there were only buildings and ridiculous streets with bright arrays of billboards flashing past the window.

"I can't find any signs to that fucking hospital!" shouted Luis.

"Calm down, Molina," said Brown. "I don't want to go to the hospital, okay? Just keep going straight." If they kept going straight, he knew, they would eventually reach the desert, because the desert was all around them.

Blood was dripping onto the floor now, having saturated the seat's fabric.

"Sorry about the mess in your car," said Brown. "I think I may have pissed myself too. I can't feel my legs anymore." Molina was shaking and couldn't think of anything to say. But there was nothing *to* say. Brown asked Stella to light a cigarette for him.

Stella's cheeks were streaked with tears. She'd grasped the situation. The filter of the cigarette she passed him was damp with her saliva, and Brown thought it was like one last kiss.

They finally left the city on one of those roads that lead nowhere, the kind of roads on which we all end up eventually.

The desert was no longer the abundance of colors it had been before; the wildflowers had already withered. Miracles, like happiness, don't last long. They're just brief instants, floating above the void.

Molina turned off the road onto a dirt track that led to a circle of rocks. The road wasn't exactly busy, but it was still better to find somewhere out of sight.

Luis cut the engine. Together, he and Stella got Brown out of the car and hauled him into the shadow of one of the rocks, his body leaving a trail of blood along the ground like a fingertip wiping a tear across a face.

"I want sunlight," gasped Brown.

They laid him down facing the light, his head resting on a large stone so he could see the earth and the sky together one last time.

"It's shitty luck to be a saint who can't even perform miracles," said Stella.

"There was nothing you could have done about that..."

Stella smiled, lit Brown a final cigarette and placed it between his lips, because she could see that this once powerful, strong-willed man was now too weak to do it himself.

Molina's phone buzzed again. He picked it up and said: "Maria..."

The others could hear the blabber of words coming from the phone, but they couldn't make out the meaning.

Luis took the phone from his ear and announced: "It's a boy."

So now Father Brown was free to die at last.

66

His body wasn't discovered until a week later, but William Bronski had known the priest was a goner as soon as the bullet hit the base of his spine. He and his brother had no doubt they would soon be receiving Brenda Moore's compliments, and that their check was already in the mail.

Now they were heading toward Los Angeles, and from there they would go to San Diego for a brief, boring vacation before they got back to work. The windshield and the wheel had been replaced and Billy was driving with one arm hanging out the window, like some poseur.

At first, they didn't understand what that dust cloud coming toward them was. The road was empty, the sky an immaculate blue, and yet this opaque mass was growing ever bigger, approaching menacingly. "What the hell is that thing?" Mike asked.

The only way to know is to see for yourself. And to penetrate the heart of things, there is no other solution: you must enter the eye of the storm.

Inside the dust cloud, they passed a hundred or so motorcyclists coming the other way along the side of the rocky road. And it was only when they emerged from the cloud, their car red with earth and the wipers frantically cleaning the windshield, that they understood.

And, as is often true in this life, they understood too late.

Comanche, standing on the footrests of his motorcycle, immobile in the middle of the road, loaded both barrels of his Winchester.

Two bullets smashed through glass, skin, and bone.

In such circumstances, life is wiped out.
And all the bad guys will be killed.

67

Luis Molina held his son in his arms, and he became a father. The sleeping baby was nestled in the crook of his elbow, and as he stared at the tiny toes sticking out from the green hospital swaddling blanket, he thought about that Rudyard Kipling poem and realized that it was wrong, that only by inverting it could you make it true: *You'll be a man, my father.*

He gently placed Luis Jr. in his crib and promised Maria he would be back in twenty-four hours. He needed to finish his work, even if it no longer had any connection to his profession, since the agency had withdrawn his press card, accusing him of inventing the entire story in the hope of winning a Pulitzer. He had enough money to last him a few months, thanks to the cash he'd found in the envelope Brown had left for him at the Days Inn in Arcadia.

He'd gone there alone, after leaving Stella *midway upon the journey of our life,* as Dante had written before beginning his voyage toward hell. "I want you to abandon me by the side of the road," she had told him. "Like a dog."

And Luis had obeyed, and Luis had arrived at this hotel in a state of total exhaustion, driven onward by his desperate desire to see his wife again and to meet his son for the first time. The receptionist had handed him the envelope containing three thousand dollars.

And the last wishes of a dead man.

But we don't care about the money. We know it's important, but we don't care about it, and it's our privilege to write that here, and even to burn it or to throw it to the wind.

Because what interests us is the parcel. Brown had written Luis a letter, explaining what to do, how it all worked, the wires that had to be connected. The letter also offered him the choice of refusing. And if he refused, he was to abandon the package by the side of the road, as he'd done with Stella.

But Luis had read the letter, cautiously opened the package, and smiled.

After that, he'd taken a shower and opened a can of Schlitz, legs stretched out on the hotel bed, and watched the last fifteen minutes of a black-and-white movie on the television in which a man was singing in the rain.

68

Washington, D.C.: the white Cadillac was stuck in the usual traffic jam on Pennsylvania Avenue.

Jeremy Carter was congratulating himself on this story's happy ending by showering Brenda Moore with compliments.

"Injecting her with chaste tree berry mixed with a narcotic... that was a stroke of genius, Brenda! Bravo!"

"It's not me you should thank, it's Gordini. It was his idea. He must have been studying his old spell books..."

"Hmm, well, it is known as the Monk's Pepper... Between you and me, though, that fat old man is not exactly the type of person to take an anaphrodisiac!"

"The effect is temporary, though. She'll start performing miracles again."

"Oh, we don't care about that. Who'd believe her now? Besides, I'm pretty sure the little slut will watch her step after all this. We won, Brenda, it's as simple as that."

He was a river in spate, monologuing compulsively. He went on to say that Simon II had personally thanked him on behalf of the College of Cardinals. The dogma was safe, and nobody would dare mess with the Christians' God any time soon. And, most importantly, he, Cardinal Carter, would be the next pope! He casually placed his slightly damp hand on Brenda's thigh, and this time, perhaps tired of having to constantly move it away, she left it where it was. Then again, perhaps it wasn't merely fatigue: perhaps this was her way of letting the cardinal enjoy one last fleeting pleasure, allowing His Eminence's hand to slide up her leg until it reached the edge of her garter, his fingertips touching the soft skin there, close to the origin of the world.

Carter closed his eyes and Brenda recognized Luis Molina when he tapped his bent index finger on the limousine's window.

"What is it?" Carter asked, a little disoriented.

Brenda lowered the electric window beside her guest. Carter did not fully remember the young man's face, and he accepted the package handed to him without understanding what was happening. "This is for you," said Luis, before disappearing into the flow of pedestrians on the sidewalk.

Brenda looked at the cardinal, then opened the car door.

"Goodbye, Carter. And good luck with the rest of your life."

She knocked on the glass divider and the chauffeur immediately got out of the car.

Carter, bewildered, watched them walk away. He stammered a few words as he held the package in his lap like a child at Christmas. This is maybe the only time I've felt even slightly sorry for him.

On the street corner, Molina took out a phone and called the number on the screen.

The detonation was not the kind that blows up half a block of houses. It was precisely the right quantity to kill the passenger sitting in the back of a car. Brown had learned that when he was a SEAL too: how to measure a dose of explosives to minimize collateral damage.

Efficiency is silence.

On another street corner, Brenda Moore lit a cigarette. Her chauffeur asked her to wait while he went to fetch a rental limousine. Molina had sent her a message a little earlier: since Brenda had spared Stella, Brown wanted her to be spared too. She stood alone, because all the other pedestrians had run as soon as they heard the explosion. In the distance, a siren was wailing.

One block away, Luis Molina tossed his phone in a trash can and began his new life as a gardener and a father.

EPILOGUE

She waited by the roadside. The sound and fury of the world was behind her.

She waited for someone to take her to the next road.

She continued the long journey of her life.

She was no longer Stella Thibodeaux. Now she was simply Stella. And there were times when she barely recognized her own reflection.

What she knew was that she was alive, and that she didn't care whether she was in America or not. Here or elsewhere, she was free. Maybe it's easier when there's space and myth to guide your steps, easier when you have the insouciance of youth to take the place of courage. That's why we should all hurry up and live.

An old Dodge pickup went past, then braked and came to a stop thirty feet away. Barefoot, hands in pockets, Stella walked toward it. Her only possession now was herself.

The boy in the truck was wearing an old pair of overalls. He had red hair, and freckles on his nose. He told her his name was Larry. He'd just turned sixteen and gotten his driver's license. When he set off, he had to let go of the steering wheel and use his left hand to shift gear.

"My right hand's paralyzed," he explained, blushing slightly. "I was born this way."

Stella looked at him. There was nothing in her pockets apart from a few dollar bills, not even her notebook.

"We can fix that, Larry. There's nothing we can't fix."